# The Break-Up Diaries

## Vol. 2

Also by Nikki Carter

*Step to This*

*It Is What It Is*

*It's All Good*

*Cool Like That*

*Not a Good Look*

*All the Wrong Moves*

*Doing My Own Thing*

Published by Kensington Publishing Corporation

# The Break-Up Diaries

## Vol. 2

## Nikki Carter
## Kevin Elliott

Dafina KTeen Books
KENSINGTON PUBLISHING CORP.
www.kensingtonbooks.com/KTeen

DAFINA KTEEN BOOKS are published by

Kensington Publishing Corp.
119 West 40th Street
New York, NY 10018

All Kensington titles, imprints, and distributed lines are
available at special quantity discounts for bulk purchases
for sales promotion, premiums, fund-raising, educational,
or institutional use.

Special book excerpts or customized printings can also
be created to fit specific needs. For details, write or
phone the office of the Kensington Special Sales Manager: Attn.: Special Sales Department. Kensington Publishing Corp., 119 West 40th Street, New York, NY 10018.
Phone: 1-800-221-2647.

K logo Reg. US Pat. & TM Off.
Sunburst logo Reg. US Pat. & TM Off.

ISBN-13: 978-0-7582-6888-4
ISBN-10: 0-7582-6888-2

First Printing: October 2011
10  9  8  7  6  5  4  3  2  1

Printed in the United States of America

# CONTENTS

# SO OVER IT

## NIKKI CARTER

# 1

It's *complicated.*

Now this is news to me. Yesterday it was not complicated at all. Just this morning, I was at the mall shopping for my boyfriend's Christmas gift. Last night, we decked the halls and sang Christmas carols at our glee club concert, and then we shared a dessert at Applebee's. It was a brownie sundae.

None of *this* was complicated!

So why are these two words in my boyfriend's Facebook profile instead of *In a Relationship*? I am perplexed, befuddled, and utterly confused.

I refresh the browser on my EVO. Yep. The offensive words are still there. Doesn't it make sense for a boyfriend to let his girlfriend know if things had become . . . complex? My eyes are wet with tears, but I won't cry yet. Not yet. I have to talk to him first.

4        The *him* that I'm referring to is my boyfriend, Mario. He is my first official boyfriend, and I can't think past a time when we won't be together.

We met our sophomore year of high school, when we both tried out for the last spot in our glee club. In my opinion, I beat him out, but our director, Ms. Rochester, couldn't decide between us, so she kept us both.

All of the other girls in glee club were immediately digging Mario, once they heard him sing. To look at him you would think he'd come with some Jonas Brothers type sound, but he's so much more soulful, like a teenage Usher. Every time he opens his mouth to sing a solo, the girls swoon.

This was okay before he became my boyfriend. It really isn't that cute now that he's my boyfriend. Well . . . I guess he's my boyfriend still.

I check my phone for missed calls. Maybe Mario was feeling some kind of way last night and couldn't get in contact with me. Perhaps he wanted to share something big and I wasn't there for him.

No missed calls.

I text my best friend, Cheyenne. Like five seconds after I click send she calls me right back. Cheyenne is not a fan of texting. It's not organic enough for her. And no, I have absolutely no idea what that means.

"Hey Cheyenne. OMG! Have you been on Facebook? Have you seen Mario's page?"

"I have."

Okay, I'm going to need my bestie's excitement level to match my frantic rave! I have an emergency going on here, and she responded like I told her that I had a peanut butter and jelly sandwich for lunch. This requires exclamation marks after sentences!

"What do you think that means?" I ask.

"Are you crying?"

"No . . . almost . . ."

Cheyenne sighs. "I think it means you need to have a conversation with Mario."

"But why do we need a conversation? Huh?"

"Your whining is excessive, Zoey. May I please wake up before I have to endure your meltdown?"

"I'm coming over. This is an emergency."

"Okay, Zoey, but we knew this was coming, right? Mario is kind of . . . a douche. You want Todrick to come too?"

Todrick is our other bestie. He's much more sympathetic than Cheyenne, so I'm thinking that, YES, I need him to come over too. Cheyenne is being way too nonchalant about this.

"Yes, Todrick is absolutely invited. Can you ask your mom to make breakfast? It feels like a French toast kind of Saturday."

"I'll ask her, but I won't make any promises."

"Okay, I'll be over in about an hour."

"Please get your whining out before you get

over here. We're going to look at the situation rationally, and then make a winning game plan."

I scrunch my nose up in confusion. "Who *are* you? I thought I called my best friend and not some infomercial life coach."

"Buster."

"Loser."

"Zoey?"

"Yeah?"

"I really feel bad that Mario broke up with you on Facebook, and you know I love you."

Is that what this is? A Facebook break up?

"Maybe we're not quite breaking up," I say with a hopeful tone in my voice that matches what I'm feeling.

"Okay. See you in a bit."


"Where are you off to so early?" my mom asks as I walk through our kitchen.

"Going over Cheyenne's for breakfast."

"Why? You can eat breakfast here."

Voting no. My mother's idea of a yummy breakfast is a wheat grass smoothie with blackberries, a banana, and protein powder. Incredibly healthy and absolutely disgusting.

I'm in the mood for something that tastes good. Yummy food will help me to feel better in case Mario really is breaking up with me.

"No thanks, mom. Mrs. Landry is making French toast. Where's dad?"

Nikki Carter

My mom frowns. "Your dad is out running. All of that sugar is not good for you Zoey."

I give her my typical blank stare. "Sugar is the world's most perfect food."

"Honey, you look sad. Is everything all right in Zoeyville?"

"Zoeyville is . . . complicated."

My mom gets up from her olive green beverage to encircle me with a hug. She's good at hugging the pain away, but for some reason it's not working this time. Mario is my first boyfriend. I don't think I can hug this away.

Even in my mind, I can't make him past tense, as in "he *was* my boyfriend."

"Is it Mario?" my mom asks, as if anything else could make me this sad.

I nod. "I think he's trying to break up with me on Facebook."

"You think? Have you talked to him?"

"No. I'm afraid to call. What if he says that he doesn't like me anymore?"

"It's always better to know than not to know."

"I was going to wait to call him until I have Cheyenne and Todrick together with me. I need them."

"I think you should do it without an audience. He might say something that you don't want to share."

My mom always has the real talk!

"Okay, I'll call him on the way over to Cheyenne's house."

I pull on a light jacket because even though it's one week away from Christmas break, I live in Texas and it is warm. Holla! That's one thing to be happy about. The temperature is about seventy degrees and the sun is shining brightly. Not swimsuit weather by any means, but there definitely isn't any snow in the forecast.

Cheyenne's house is a five minute walk from mine, but I don't mind walking because the weather is so nice.

I hesitate to call Mario, but then decide that my mother's advice is usually the best.

I press his name from the Call Log, and his phone only rings once before he answers.

"Hey Zoey. I know why you're calling me."

"You do?"

"Yeah, and we kinda need to talk."

I desperately, frantically search for some friendliness in his voice, but it's not there. He sounds almost mean, like he'd rather be doing anything other than talk to me.

"Okay . . . what do we need to talk about?"

"I think we should start dating other people."

I feel my steps quicken and my heart race. Is this what an anxiety attack feels like? I'm too young for those.

"And do you already have someone in mind?" I ask.

Mario pauses. And it's way too long. Whatever he's about to say next is probably a lie.

"My dad says a boy in the eleventh grade shouldn't be tied to one girl."

Wow. This is worse than a lie. This is a mini-speech and a poorly constructed one at that.

"I thought your dad liked me."

"He does, but he thinks you're clingy."

He thinks I'm *clingy*. What in the world? I think I can be described as many things, but not clingy.

"So he thinks you should date someone else?"

"Yeah, pretty much."

"So are you breaking up with me?"

This comes out sounding like a whine. Like something a clingy girl would say. But I can't help it. Tears are streaming down my face, but he's so cool about this! How can he be so cool about this?

"I think we just shouldn't date. I don't know if it's officially, like, a break up. I'm not mad at you or anything. But I agree with my dad."

"Can I ask who you're going to start dating?"

I can hear his sigh through the phone. He's got no right to be frustrated. He's the one breaking up with *me*. I should be the one with the angst.

"Come on Zoey," he says. "You don't want to do this. Let's just see one another at school and stuff."

But I just spent a large chunk of my Christmas money buying him a Fossil watch and two T-shirts from Hollister. It's a good thing I kept the receipts.

I bet he didn't even buy me anything.

"Um . . . Zoey, can I talk to you later? I've got basketball practice, and . . . really . . . I don't have anything else to say."

"Okay . . ."

Then he just disconnects the call, like we haven't been dating since the summer. My chest feels heavy, like I've got an elephant sitting on me.

My tears form a nasty combination liquid with my snot that dribbles down my chin. I just want to sit on this curb and bawl my eyes out. Maybe if I cry loud enough and hard enough, Mario will hear me and change his mind about this foolishness.

But Cheyenne sees me sitting outside. She's looking from her living room window. I can see her expression of concern from where I'm sitting. Next thing I know she's running across her yard, with her wild, curly golden brown afro blowing in the wind.

"What's wrong?" Cheyenne asks. Then she answers for herself. "You talked to him didn't you."

I nod. "He said he wants to date other people."

The tears that had started to slow begin all over again.

"Come inside," Cheyenne says. "The French toast is ready and we don't want Todrick to eat it all."

A little smile graces my face. I'm not surprised that Todrick beat me here. He lives next door to Cheyenne, and he loves breakfast.

As soon as I step into the house, Cheyenne's mom, Ms. Brandi (she only lets us call her by her first name) sits a plate in front of me. My empty stomach grumbles with anticipation of the perfectly golden French toast, carmelized bananas, and pure maple syrup. The entire house smells heavenly from the sweet and sugary breakfast treat.

I take a huge bite of my food. It is sooo good! So good that just for a second I forget all about Mario's torturous activities.

Todrick grins at me as he takes the last bite on his plate. "Delicious, right?"

"Ridiculously so. Ms. Brandi, you should open a restaurant," I say. "All French toast all the time."

"Don't forget the scrambled eggs with cheese!" Todrick exclaims.

Ms. Brandi laughs. "This is why I love you two. Cheyenne never lets me feed her properly."

Cheyenne fakes a gag. "I will take a fruit smoothie over that lard filled mess any day."

I tilt my head to one side, so that my perfectly trimmed, pin straight hair swishes. "Ms. Brandi, I think Cheyenne and I were switched at birth. My mom is drinking seaweed and spinach right now, as we speak!"

Ms. Brandi frowns. "Yuck."

"Exactly," I reply.

"Are we going to cease with the chit-chat about unhealthy versus healthy breakfast and get to the reason why we're here?" Cheyenne asks impatiently. "Mom can you please leave us? This is not fit for your ears."

Ms. Brandi bursts into laughter. "Y'all drama is not even *that* serious! I got some real drama for you."

"Unfortunately, right now we've got to deal with the mess of devastation that is Zoey," Cheyenne responds.

Wow. Way to bring me back to reality. I was enjoying the pretending! I'm pretending not to even think about Mario and break up in the same sentence. Boo, Cheyenne! Boo!

"I heard on Friday," Todrick says after Ms. Brandi exits, "after the glee club concert."

I drop my fork. "You heard my boyfriend was breaking up with me on *Friday* and you didn't say anything? How could you Todrick!"

Todrick gives me an apologetic look as he runs the hand not holding the fork through his thick, black curly hair.

"I didn't want to say anything until I knew for sure. I didn't hear Mario say it. It was Dorie."

Dorie McMichael. Grrrr. She's the basketball cheerleader/honors student/glee club soloist that *all* the guys want.

Did Mario break up with me for Dorie? This would make it even worse! I'll never be able to show my face in school again.

"*She's* dating him now?" I ask.

Todrick shrugs. "At least it's not a downgrade. That would be worse."

Cheyenne says, "Stop. We don't care who Mario has chosen to date."

"We don't?" I ask.

I'm confused. How am I going to get him back if I don't know who he's dating now? Although if he's dating Dorie, my chances are basically slim to none. What am I going to do?

"No. We don't care because he no longer matters. He is the past," Cheyenne declares.

Just this morning, he was the present. What a difference a few hours and a random Facebook post make.

"But I don't want him to be the past," I say. "I want to know how to get him back."

Todrick asks, "Why do you want him back if he played you?"

"He *played* me? Are you saying that he got with Dorie *before* we broke up? I'm up here thinking he's breaking up with me to go out with Dorie!"

Cheyenne gives Todrick an evil glare and he stares down into his plate. The red tone creeping up his neck to his cheeks tells me that he's embarrassed by his diarrhea of the mouth.

"Todrick . . . you better tell me. Who do you want angry at you? Me or Cheyenne?" I ask.

"Actually, I'm more scared of Cheyenne. She hits like a man."

Cheyenne interjects. "You know what, Todrick?

Tell her. She needs to hear the dirty truth. I have a feeling she's not going to get over this crap or that loser until she knows everything."

"Mario is not a loser. You take that back, Cheyenne!"

"Zoey, I will not take it back. And you'll agree with me once you know the truth. Spill it, Todrick!"

Todrick looks at Cheyenne skeptically before he begins. I know why, too. She's been known to change her mind after making one of her declarations.

"Well . . . I *heard* that he started light weight kicking it with Dorie over Thanksgiving."

I feel my mood darken further if this is even possible. Thanksgiving was when I went with my parents and bratty little sister to Houston. We had dinner at my non-cooking aunt Tina's house. While I was eating dry turkey and lumpy mashed potatoes, Mario was getting with whore-y Dorie.

"So he's probably lying about his father saying that I'm clingy . . . huh?"

"Probably. I think he's been lying about everything," Cheyenne says.

Lying about everything? Does that include all the times he told me that I'm pretty or that I could be his best friend? What about when he gave me this bracelet with a key charm and told me, "Now you have the key to my heart."

Were all of those lies too?

Tears start again and splash down into my

plate. It doesn't matter anyway because I couldn't eat another bite if I tried.

"What am I going to do now?" I ask between sobs.

"First, you're going to stop crying," Cheyenne says.

"I am?"

"Yes. You are."

I take in a huge breath and try to sit up taller in my seat. I want to be able to follow these instructions. Maybe they'll make me feel better.

"Then," Cheyenne continues, "you're going to purge yourself of all things Mario."

I'm not sure I know what she means by *purging*. Purging sounds drastic and final. I am not ready for purging. I don't care what Cheyenne says.

"I don't want to purge him! I *love* him!"

Cheyenne grabs my wrist and unsnaps my bracelet. Then, she tosses it in the trash can.

"Cheyenne! Mario gave me that for my birthday!"

"Oh, stop with the crying!" Cheyenne fusses. "He spent three bucks on it at Claire's!"

Todrick swallows another bite of food and says, "This is going to be a long day."

I agree with him. This feels like the longest, most awful, incredibly heartbreaking day of my life. And it's only ten o'clock in the morning.

How am I going to make it through the rest of the day?

# 2

Cheyenne, Todrick, and I are back at my house. We're in my bedroom, staring at a pile of gifts from Mario. Cheyenne is holding a box in her hand and wearing a scowl on her face. I think she's still mad that I fished the bracelet out of her trash. What-the-heck-ever!

"Okay, hand over all of the Mario paraphernalia," Cheyenne says.

I am utterly skeptical of this. "What are you going to do with it?" I ask.

"Well, since you dang near put me in a choke hold to save that cheap bracelet, we're just going to put everything Mario related in this box."

"Then what?" I ask.

"Then we will store the items in a neutral location until you are willing to be rational about Mario."

I cross my arms and plop down on my bed. *"Your* house is not a neutral location."

"Okay," Cheyenne says as she hands the box to Todrick. "We'll put the contraband at Todrick's house."

"Gifts from my boyfriend are not contraband!"

Todrick touches my arm lightly. "He's not your boyfriend anymore. He's your ex-boyfriend, Zoey. You should probably get used to saying that."

"No. I think that maybe we're just overreacting. When I asked him if he was breaking up with me, he didn't come out and say yes," I explain. "I think he's on the fence about it."

"She's in denial," Cheyenne says.

"Just hear me out!" I say. "Maybe . . . just maybe he's feeling some kind of way about us. Maybe he's afraid of how deeply we feel about one another."

Big sigh from Cheyenne. Who does she think she is sighing at me? I don't get frustrated when she tries to force all of her organic, vegan products on me. So, how is she soooo annoyed when I've got a real problem going on?

"Let's go," Cheyenne says.

"Where are we going?" Todrick asks.

"Dorie and her whole crew are supposed to be at GoKart Heaven this afternoon," Cheyenne explains.

"And how do you know the comings and goings of Dorie?" I ask suspiciously.

"My kid brother Marcus is her brother Ethan's bestie. There's a birthday party for Ethan, and he's annoyed that Dorie is coming and bringing her friends."

I consider this outing. If Dorie is there, with Mario, I will probably freak out. I don't know how I'll be able to handle that. I haven't broken up with Mario. Not in my brain and definitely not in my heart.

"I don't think this is a good idea," I say.

"Do you want to know the truth or not?" Cheyenne asks.

"If the truth has anything to do with Mario dating Dorie, then no."

My cell phone buzzes on the bed. I reach out to grab it, but Cheyenne beats me to it.

She reads the text aloud. "Hope you are okay— Mario."

My heart soars! I know that Mario still cares about me. He's just feeling a little confused right now. That's why he put "it's complicated" instead of "single" on his Facebook status. Why shouldn't he get to feel this way? We're teenagers for crying out loud. I feel confused about stuff all the time.

I feel my sadness evaporate like a pan full of hot dog water.

"Take that, Cheyenne. I told you we were going to work things out."

"First of all, you're not going to answer this text. Second of all, I don't think this means anything other than the fact that he's guilty. It probably makes him feel weird to think about you crying over him!"

Todrick asks, "Are we going to GoKart Heaven? It sounds like fun."

Cheyenne cuts her eyes at Todrick, and he says, "I mean it would sound like fun if we weren't going to catch Mario in the act of playing you."

"Okay, I'll go," I say. "But I won't like it."

"Cool," Cheyenne replies. "Let's pick out an outfit."

I look down at my T-shirt, cargo pants, and Chuck Taylor Converse sneakers. This is standard kicking it gear as far as I'm concerned.

"What is wrong with what I'm wearing?" I ask. "It's perfect for go-kart racing."

"Your outfit is being planned for Mario, not a go-kart. And it's got to be hot."

Todrick scrunches his nose into a frown. "Why would she be getting all dolled up for Mario? I thought we were helping her get over him, not trying to get him back. I'm not understanding."

Cheyenne replies, "She's not trying to win him back. She's making him realize what he lost. You are not supposed to understand. You are supposed to observe."

"Well, if he's comparing my looks to Dorie's, I don't have a chance. She's got a great body and mine hasn't grown in yet. Plus she's popular. Who am I kidding?"

"No ma'am," Cheyenne says. "Nobody cares

20

about having a chance because you aren't getting back with him. And you are not going to sit here and get down on yourself. You are smart and pretty. You're popular, too!"

Cheyenne walks over to my closet and flings the door open. Todrick and I watch in awe as she rifles through my closet, pulling out clothes. She mutters angrily as she puts together ensembles.

Man, Cheyenne is serious about this.

Todrick says, "Cheyenne, you're so angry! It's like he broke up with you or something."

Cheyenne replies, "I just hate jerks like Mario. They get all the girls and nobody holds them responsible for all the people they hurt."

Talk about taking it personal.

After looking at a few options, Cheyenne holds up a cute khaki skirt, cream leggings, a brown and gold baby tee, and a jean jacket. I can rock with this. Definitely fiyah!

"Okay, I'll change. But Cheyenne, can I ask you a favor?"

"What is it?"

"Can you please not act all charged up when we go to GoKart Heaven? I don't roll like that."

Cheyenne lifts an eyebrow. "If you see what I think you're gonna see, I'm gonna be the one holding you back."

I shrug off Cheyenne's warning. I believe what they are telling me about Dorie. Todrick wouldn't say anything like that if he didn't absolutely know for sure.

I grab my cute outfit and run into my bathroom to change. I look in the mirror and am not thrilled about my red, puffy and swollen face. This will not do at all. I take a cool face cloth and press it against my eyes, hoping that the swelling will go down some.

I've got to look completely chill and cool and pretty and fresh to death. All of the things that make me Zoey.

Because, my plan, no matter what Cheyenne says, is to convince my boyfriend, the one that I love, that we should still be together. If I put my game face on, it shouldn't be all that hard . . . I hope.

# 3

GoKart Heaven used to be one of my favorite places to hang out when I was in middle school. The food is awesome! They have cheddar bacon fries, hot wings, pizza, milkshakes, and a bunch of other perfectly prepared junk foods! All the stuff we love for our pig out sessions. And they have six humongous go-kart race tracks. Some are for beginners, some for the bit more advanced, and some for the daredevils. I've done them all!

I have *great* memories from here! And I'm hoping to keep all of them intact.

Cheyenne, Todrick, Cheyenne's little brother Marcus, and I walk up to the ticket counter to purchase our tickets for the rides. I feel nervousness in the pit of my stomach at what could happen next. I hate feeling nervous.

If I see Mario here with Dorie, I will remain calm. I will ride the go-karts a few times. I will split some fries with Todrick, and then I'll go home to lick my wounds. Maybe, I'll even change my Facebook status!

*That* is the plan.

We walk indoors to the table area where they set up the birthday parties for little kids. Marcus takes off running with his little birthday present for Ethan.

Dorie is helping her mom set plates out in front of the kids. Pretending that she's a nice person who helps her mom. Yeah, right. If I see her with Mario, I won't have anything nice to say about her. She'll be nothing but a boyfriend-stealer to me.

Everyone in glee club knows we're together. We sit together on every bus trip. I decorated his locker for his birthday. He gave me a singing telegram for mine. Everyone thought it was cute.

Everybody knows. Including Dorie. So if she's kicking it with Mario, this makes her a boyfriend-stealer.

I can't say that I'm friends with Dorie, though. That would make it much worse, I guess. If she was my friend, I'd be losing a boyfriend and a bestie.

But, I'm getting ahead of myself. I haven't lost anyone or anything yet. Because until I see it with my own eyes, I'm still in the game.

Now Dorie is waving for us to come over to the table. She's got a huge smile on her face like she's happy to see us. That's funny, because I'm feeling quite the opposite about her right now.

"What the what?" Cheyenne asks. "Why is she trying to play like we're cool, when we so obviously are not?"

"Yeah," Todrick adds. "This is *Twilight Zone* type stuff."

Actually, this makes me feel good. If Dorie's being so friendly toward us, then maybe she's not trying to be that chick that stole my boyfriend.

"Cheyenne!" Dorie squeals as we approach. "Thank you so much for bringing your brother! He and Ethan are so close."

She sounds ridiculously bubbly. Too bubbly if you ask me. This makes me extremely suspicious.

"Hey Dorie," I say. "Happy Birthday, Ethan."

Both Cheyenne and Todrick wave without saying anything. I guess I'm more willing to give her the benefit of the doubt than they are.

Dorie's little brother just stares at me like he wants to yell out, "Stranger danger!" or something.

Then Ethan says, "See, Mom! Why are Dorie's friends here?"

Dorie's mother looks at us and squints. Then, she pats little Ethan on the back.

"Oh, honey, these aren't Dorie's friends. They're just people she knows from school. They're dropping Marcus off. Isn't that right?"

Wow! Way to let us know that we're not welcome. Apparently Dorie gets her clique behavior honestly. I don't think I've ever seen someone's mom be so rude.

Cheyenne says, "Come on y'all. Let's go get some food."

We go to the snack counter and place our orders for fries and pizza and then take a seat in front of the counter to wait. Everything at GoKart Heaven is cooked to order. That's why it tastes so good.

OMG! I just sounded like a random commercial.

"Dorie's mother is rude," Todrick says. "She didn't even want Dorie to introduce us."

"Yeah! Really rude, especially since I was in Girl Scouts with Dorie for all of elementary school," Cheyenne says. "She and my mother had a fight one year over some Thin Mints and it was all over. She probably hates that her son is in my dad's Boy Scout troop. That's how Ethan and Marcus got to be friends."

Todrick laughs out loud. "Thank you for giving us all this hater history *before* we went over to meet the lady!"

I join in the laughter. "I'm just trying to figure out why Dorie called us over to the table. It's like she knew her mother was gonna front or say something crazy. Maybe that's what she wanted."

Cheyenne waves a hand in the air. "Dorie's

skanky mama is irrelevant. Let's stay on task here."

"Dang!" Todrick exclaims. "You called Dorie's mother skanky! Harsh!"

"Listen here!" Cheyenne fusses. "We are not about to debate whether or not Dorie's mother is a skank. We're waiting for Mario to show up."

"He's not coming," I say. "Because I've got a feeling he's still into me. All the gossip y'all heard was just that. Gossip."

Our food is ready and Todrick goes to the counter to get our trays. Cheyenne watches Dorie's group like a hawk, but I only glance over in their direction every few minutes or so. I don't want to seem like we're here stalking them, but apparently Cheyenne doesn't care what they think.

Dorie's cheerleader friends stream in one by one, all wearing our school colors, black and gold. They all look so pretty and perfect with their high ponytails, ribbons, and bear paw face paint. Just like a Disney movie or something.

"I can't stand them," Cheyenne says. "They think they're all that, and they're really just a bunch of fakers."

"They look pretty real to me," I reply.

Todrick sets our food down on the table, and rubs his hands together. "I hope y'all are hungry, and if you're not I can finish what you don't eat."

I thought I was hungry, but as soon as I saw the pretty perfects walk up in the spot, my stomach started doing flip-flops. Now, I don't know if I want any food. Actually, I feel those random bites of French toast churning like a miniature tornado in my midsection. This is not a good thing.

"Go ahead," I say. "Chow down on the fries. If I get hungry later, I'll grab some."

So far, no Mario, and that's good. There are some boys with their group now, but none of them are Mario's friends so I'm feeling good about that. To keep from looking at them, I watch Todrick vaporize the food like it's his last meal on planet Earth.

"Isn't there anyone else you have a crush on?" Todrick asks. "I mean, I feel kind of like a stalker, waiting for Mario to show up. If he wants things to be *complicated*, I don't see why you can't just be on to the next one."

Cheyenne gives him a high five across the table. "That's the first great thing you've said all day Todrick. She should just kick this buster to the curb and start digging on someone else. That's the most logical thing to do."

I shake my head. "Y'all don't know Mario like I do! He's the only guy I'd want to kick it with right now. I've already planned out our prom colors. I'm wearing teal and he's wearing white. We've even talked about college. We're either going to go to Texas A & M or Prairie View, unless he gets a basketball scholarship somewhere. With my grades, I can go wherever I want. So we'll be able to be together no matter what."

Cheyenne and Todrick stare at each other and then back at me.

"What? There is nothing wrong with planning for the future. That's why so many young people look up their senior year and they don't know what they're going to do. I am a planner. That's what I do. And there is nothing wrong with that. Even though y'all are looking at me crazy. I don't care about y'all looking at me like that."

Blank, silent stares from both of them.

Then finally Cheyenne says, "This is unhealthy."

I'm unhealthy? Wow, okay. Cheyenne calling me unhealthy is like the pot calling the kettle black. It's not very healthy how she pushes every boy away like they have the plague. She doesn't trust anyone! She thinks every boy has one prime directive—to hook up. And true enough most of them do, not *all* of them are the same. Mario never pressured me at all.

Todrick lets out a small belch. "That was delicious. Can we go ride some go-karts?"

"Rude! And yes, this staring at Dorie and her lame-o friends is getting on my nerves," Cheyenne says. "I need a change of scenery."

We toss the remaining crumbs into the trash and head outdoors to the go-kart tracks. We pick one of the intermediate tracks to start, and then we'll work our way up. The line is pretty long, so we get in it, before a rush of kids comes out of the food court and makes us have to wait even longer.

"How are you feeling?" Todrick asks me as the line progresses. "You look a little stressed."

"Ya think? I just want this whole thing to be some nightmare I'm having. Any moment I'll wake up."

Cheyenne says, "Usually, I can tell when I'm having a dream, because all types of weird stuff is taking place. It's like my body wants me to know I'm dreaming."

"Like what?" Todrick asks.

"Okay, for example, if I have to use the bathroom while I'm dreaming, in the dream, I'm walking around looking for a bathroom. But I can never find one that has a closed door. Like it's always something where people can see me, so I never go."

I burst into laughter. "That's your body trying to keep you from peeing in the bed!"

All three of us crack up laughing. Just like this is any other Christmas break day. But it isn't really just any other day, is it?

"Are you getting cash for Christmas?" I ask Todrick. "I asked for money and gift cards."

"Me too," Todrick says. "Hopefully I got some kind of game system, too, and a gift card to Game Stop. Holla at ya' boy!"

Cheyenne sucks her teeth. "You two are so materialistic."

"What did you ask for?" Todrick asks.

"Nothing. My mom knows what I like. I'll be happy with whatever I get."

I roll my eyes. "You kill me acting like you're so much more mature than us. You like Hollister T-shirts too. Stop acting like you don't want gift cards."

Cheyenne giggles. "I didn't say I don't want them. I just never ask for anything. Then my mother thinks I'm all about the spirit behind giving. In turn, I get *more* stuff. Get hip to the game!"

More laughing from us, and I'm glad we're having so much fun, because the line seems to be moving much faster with us shooting the breeze.

Then it happens.

The exact thing that I was convinced wouldn't happen.

Dorie and Mario walk out to the go-kart line, arm and arm.

My stomach drops and I swallow a mouthful of spit. Cheyenne and Todrick don't see them yet. But they both stare at me. I probably look like a statue, frozen in time, because I cannot move. Cheyenne follows my eyes with her own.

"Oh crap," she says. "The jerk has made his appearance."

Dorie and Mario don't want to wait in line, so they get in front of some of their friends. I hear Dorie saying to the people at the end of the line, "Sorry, we're all together."

I don't want them riding the same time as me. I don't want them anywhere near me. I don't want them on the same planet as me.

"You can take number fifteen." The go-kart attendant is talking to me, but it's like his voice is in a vacuum. I can barely hear what he's saying, and it sounds like he's speaking in slow motion.

Cheyenne drags me to the go-kart and helps me get in. "Are you okay?" she asks. "Because we can just leave."

I smile up at her. "I'm cool."

"You sure?"

I nod slowly. "I'm sure, I'm sure!"

I am sooo not sure.

Mario walks right past me, holding hands with Dorie, as they go to two go-karts of the row next to mine. I feel a wave of sadness sweep over me. It feels like a blanket on a summer night. Totally uncomfortable.

How could they be at the holding hand stage already? It took us forever to get there. Well, at least two months. How long has he been creeping with her?

OMG! Why did this chick just kiss my boyfriend on the cheek before she gets in her go-kart? This is utterly ridiculous. Either they're putting on a show, or they are for real.

Either way, I feel this sadness morph into something else. That something else has my blood feeling like it's about to evaporate. I've never been so furious in my life. All because I saw a little kiss on the cheek.

"Hey, Zoey," Mario calls from his go-kart. "I didn't know you'd be here."

Hey? Hey! He's going to act all nonchalant like

he didn't just stick a knife in my heart and twist it? I can't believe that this is the person that I spent half of my Christmas money on. I should've bought something for myself.

I hear the starting gun pop, and I floor the gas pedal in my go-kart. I channel all of my rage into my foot, like I want to press the thing all the way through the floor.

There's a red haze in front of my eyes, and I only want to do one thing . . . ram this go-kart right into the back of Mario. If I can get Dorie too, it'll be great, but my first target is Mario.

Mario who lied to me. Lied and said he was my best friend. Lied and said his father thinks I'm clingy. There is *no way* his father said that.

I cannot stand Mario right now.

A hot tear blows out of the corner of my eye and into the wind. I'm going so fast that it doesn't even have time to trickle down my face.

Mario must feel that I'm in hot pursuit of him, because he puts the pedal to the metal too. He's a few car lengths ahead of me, but I know I can catch him. I've got to be able to catch him. With so many other things going wrong for me today this has to go right.

I've got his *complicated*! Complicated! There is nothing complicated about what he did. He lied and pretended to be my boyfriend while he was creeping with Dorie for who knows how long.

Doesn't sound too complex to me! Actually, it sounds pretty simple. And I'm simply about to put the front end of this go-kart, right into the back of his! That'll teach him.

I turn the wheel to the right and slide past a little kid who's in my path to smashing Mario. Move! Get out the way!

Now, I'm just one car behind him. Right within smashing space. I'm going to get him, and it's not going to be pretty. I chuckle to myself when I think of his go-kart and the ruined tires on the side. They'll have to walk him off the track like they do the little kids that crash and burn. He won't be hurt, but he'll be embarrassed.

And maybe that will make him feel just a little bit like how I feel.

Because more than anything, this is humiliating.

Everyone knows we were together. And then he would just show up somewhere holding hands with Dorie? He could've at least given me time to get over it, before he went public with his new chick.

Now, I'm right on his tail. There is no escaping my wrath. The backside of that go-kart is about to feel the pain! I press the pedal hard and feel that extra burst of speed. It's like I've got a turbo boost button. All the better to ram you with my dear ex-boyfriend!

I'm so focused on tearing Mario up, that I don't realize I'm coming up on a curve. He rounds it effortlessly, because his go-kart is not flying by at its maximum speed. I, however, am in no position to slow down. I try lifting my foot off the gas, because if I hit the brake, I'm going to go skidding across the track.

Unfortunately, lifting my foot off the gas does absolutely nothing to slow me down. I think my go-kart is being powered on pure anger. I can't even feel the wheels touching the track right now.

Why can't I feel the wheels on the track?

OMG! My go-kart is airborne!

After a few seconds that feel like forever, I hit the track with a thud and spin out in the middle of the track. After about four spins, I do exactly what I wanted Mario to do . . . wipe out in the tires on the side of the track.

This totally sucks.

Now the top of my go-kart is smoking like one of the race cars on NASCAR. The attendant blows a whistle and waves traffic away from me as he runs out to save me. Tears stream down my face. No, I'm not hurt. I'm mad that I didn't get Mario.

When the attendant gets to me he screams, "What the heck are you doing? Are you trying to kill yourself out here? You are totally not driving in a safe manner!"

I just look at him, and wonder if he ever thought in a million years if this was where he'd be working after he graduated high school. A place where a bunch of raggedy teenagers try to ram each other with go-karts when they go kissing their new girlfriend in public when they were only your boyfriend just yesterday!

AAARRRRGGGGHHH!

"Come on," the attendant fusses. "Out of the go-kart."

I step out of the wounded contraption gingerly. The smoke rising up from the wreckage hurts my eyes, and the track is super slippery so I hold the attendant's arm when he holds it out to me. I'm starting to think that these ballerina slippers were not the most practical choice of shoe to wear go-kart racing. But that's what happens when you let someone else pick your outfit.

I hear people laughing as I slip and slide off the track. Someone yells, "Wipe out!" I scowl in the general direction of the shout. Mario better be glad it doesn't sound like him.

The attendant sees someone start to press the gas on their go-kart and he yanks his arm away from me to give them the signal to stop! As he yanks his arm away, he literally propels me across the slippery track. Just like my go-kart, there is no way for me to slow myself without crashing and burning. But this time, I end up on my behind in the middle of the track instead of in the tires.

"Get her off the track!" Someone screams.

The attendant looks at me and frowns. Then he practically drags me off the track, holding one of my arms and one of my feet. I'm almost one hundred percent sure that this is not protocol.

I glance over at the go-kart riders and feel so ashamed. My cream leggings are now all skidded up with the dirt from the track and my wrist and ankle are sore from where the crazy attendant dragged me off the track.

Then, horror of horrors. I look up and see Dorie taking a video of the whole thing with her iPhone. Could this day get any worse?

Cheyenne and Todrick both abandon their go-karts and follow me off the track. They take their time walking, but Todrick has on Timberland boots and Cheyenne has on sneakers, so they're not slipping at all. I'm the only nutsy noo-noo with ballerina shoes on.

Once I'm off the track, I make a beeline for the door. I hope that Cheyenne and Todrick are behind me. We get to Cheyenne's car and I hear her click the locks open.

I jump into the back seat and as soon as I plop down, my sobs start. Horrible, loud, ugly noises that scare me. This is the worst day ever. Someday, I'll probably look back on all this and have a good laugh. But it won't be today. It won't be this week and it won't be this year.

Cheyenne sticks her head in the door. "I'm so sorry, Zoey. I've got to go and get my little brother, but after that we can leave."

"Th-thank you," I say.

Todrick slides into the backseat next to me and puts his arm around my shoulder. He pulls my head into his chest and moves the hair out of my eyes, while I cry.

"Try to pull yourself together in case they come out here," he says. "You don't want Mario and Dorie to see you like this."

Right now, I don't care who sees me like what. This has got to be a dream, right? Things this ridiculous only happen in dreams.

"Pinch me," I say to Todrick.

"Huh?" he says. "Oh . . . I'm sorry, Zoey. You are wide awake."

Worst. Day. Ever.

# 4

haven't come out of my bedroom since the go-kart incident. Both my mom and my dad fussed at me for the stunt. They both told me I could've been killed. They both said that they had no idea what I was thinking. My mom said she was ashamed of my actions. My dad said that I'm grounded until he forgets what I did.

Blah, blah, blah, whatever.

When they asked me why I ignored all of the safety rules of GoKart Heaven and drove like a maniac, there was nothing I could say. And the manager of GoKart Heaven made sure to tell my mother that if I ever tried something like that again, I would be banned from their facility and that she and my dad would get a fine.

So, yeah, I'll probably be grounded until college. But who cares about being grounded? I never want to go out of my room again anyway, so they can do all the grounding they want. I really don't care.

My mom threatened to take all my Christmas presents back. Christmas is in three days. Looks like I might not get to have my shopping spree. But who cares about shopping when I'll never need a new outfit again?

I pull the covers up to my neck and close my eyes. This bed is the only sanctuary I have right now. I snuggle down into the warm spot that I've made from being here for the last twenty-four hours.

I hear a knock at my bedroom door. "Mom says that it's time to eat!" my sister says.

"Not hungry!" I yell at the door.

I can tell she's still standing there because I can hear her breathing.

"Go away!" I shout. "I don't want anything to eat."

"Mom says that you have to come down anyway. She said you can't stay in your bed forever."

I let out a big sigh. I know if I don't go downstairs and show my face, that she's just going to come up here and annoy me even more.

I stand up and wrap my comforter around my body. I don't stop to brush my teeth or smooth my hair which is standing up in the air. I put on my glasses, because I've been crying too hard to put in my contacts.

When I get to the dining room, my little sister takes one look at me and bursts out laughing.

"Mom!" I say.

"Layla, stop laughing at your sister."

"But she looks like the creature from the black lagoon!"

My mother looks me up and down and frowns. "Zoey, you do look a hot mess. I'm giving you some green tea. I think you need a laxative, too."

A laxative? Why does she think that getting rid of poop is the cure to every ill in the world? I do not need a laxative for crying out loud! My boyfriend dumped me for a big-booty cheer-leader!

My dad is the only one who shows me any pity. He genuinely looks sad for me.

"Zoey, go on back upstairs. I'll bring you a sandwich later," he says.

My mother glares at him, but I run over and give him a hug. My daddy! My hero! At least this proves that not every male on the planet is evil.

"Zoey," my daddy says, "please brush your teeth when you go back upstairs, your breath smells like a sewer plant."

I blow some breath in my hand and smell it. Whew! He's right. Raw sewage. Maybe I do need a laxative.

Once I'm back upstairs, I do brush my teeth, but then I get right back into my still warm spot on the bed. I take out my cell phone and with much trepidation, I pull up Mario's Facebook page. I'm afraid of what I'll see, but some morbid thing on the inside of me makes me check it anyway.

Involuntary tears spring to my eyes when I see his wall. Now his status says, "In a Relationship". And guess who hit the 'like' button. Exactly. Miss Big Booty Cheerleader herself. Dorie.

How in the heck can they be in a relationship? They're just using that word too randomly for me. A relationship happens once you get to know someone, and you realize that everything you say around them is okay, because they totally get you. And that sometimes it's okay to not say anything because you're comfortable just chilling in each other's company.

A relationship is what I thought Mario and I had. I was wrong. I think I was in a relationship, but he was not. And that's the other thing about a *relationship*. It's got to involve more than one person.

I remember the first time Mario asked me to be his girlfriend. It was at the end of last school year, our tenth grade year. We were on the bus, coming back from a glee club competition. We lost, but we were all still in a pretty good mood because we did our best. We're really good sports about stuff like that.

But anyway, I was eating a Snickers candy bar, when Mario asked me, "Can I get a bite of your candy?"

"No!" I said. "Hungry here! This is my only dinner. I didn't get to eat before we left the school."

He slid in the seat next to me, which made me kind of nervous. I'd been out a few times with Mario and some other people from glee club, and he seemed cool. He also seemed like he was digging me, but I couldn't be sure. Neither Cheyenne nor Todrick were there for me to bounce any ideas on, so I just went with what I was feeling.

"I bet if I were your boyfriend, you'd let me share," Mario said.

"Maybe. But if you were my boyfriend, wouldn't you care that I hadn't eaten since lunch? Wouldn't you want me to enjoy my candy bar?"

Mario shrugged. "Maybe I would. But boys are pretty selfish. I'd want some just to say I got my girlfriend to share. It would make me feel like a man."

I laughed out loud. "But you're not a man. You're a tenth grader."

"That's almost the same thing. So are you going to give me a bite?" he asked.

I took a big bite of my candy bar and chewed. "Nope. You're not my boyfriend."

Suddenly, Mario stopped laughing and gave me a serious look. "Do you want me to be?"

I almost choked on my candy bar. He was staring at me so hard that I thought he was going to bite me instead of the Snickers.

"Are you for real?" I asked.

"If I was would you say yes?"

I swallowed the candy and tried to read his face for a clue that he was playing or tripping. But he just grinned at me and kept staring.

So I shrugged and replied, "If you were serious, I'd probably say yes."

He laughed. "What do I have to do to get the probably into the definite category?"

"You'd just have to come out and ask me, without the games, I guess."

Mario got up from the seat then, and went back to the rear of the bus with his friends. He said, "Enjoy your candy bar," as he walked away.

The entire ride back to the school I thought about our conversation, and it made me feel warm inside. I definitely wanted him to be my boyfriend, and I hoped, hoped, hoped that he'd ask me again . . . the right way.

As we got off the bus, I listened to Mario joke with his boys. Someone made a fart joke that had gone on entirely too long. I guessed that the moment was over. Maybe he'd had a lapse of insanity and didn't really mean what he'd said about the whole boyfriend request.

We all waited outside for our parents to pick us up. We were back from the competition early. We were supposed to be picked up by nine o'clock, but it was only eight thirty. Since neither Cheyenne nor Todrick is in glee club I just chilled by myself on the curb.

I remember sending Cheyenne a text. *I think Mario likes me.*

Her response was: *He's a jerk and a player. Tell him to step.*

As I was reading her reply and laughing, Mario sat down next to me. "What's so funny?" he asked.

"Nothing. My friend said something cute."

He lifted one eyebrow and grinned. Oh, how I loved when he made that face at me. That was his cutest face!

"Was it a text from your boyfriend? Is that why you're giving me such a hard time?" he asked.

I feigned innocence. "Me! I'm not giving you a hard time. I answered all of your questions."

"Okay, you're right. You did. So, now, I'm asking you for real. Will you be my girlfriend? I really like you, Zoey."

I gulped, and looked down at Cheyenne's text. What did she know anyway? If I knew then what I know now, I would've listened to Cheyenne and her wise text. But at the time, I wasn't thinking about wisdom. I was thinking about having my first boyfriend.

And that he was gorgeous! His dark hair was in a low hair cut, but it covered his head in thick waves. Then his eyelashes were so long that they brushed his cheek when he blinked. I honestly was surprised that he was interested in me. I wondered what he saw in me.

Then he told me. "You're pretty, but you don't

go around acting like you're the stuff, you know. You're nice to everybody, and that's hot. So, I want to kick it with you."

I could barely get the words out when I replied, "I want to kick it with you too."

But all of that is over now. It seems like it happened so long ago. I just kills me that I didn't see any signs.

Like shouldn't you be able to tell when someone doesn't like you anymore?

I send Cheyenne a text. :(

She sends me one back. *I kno. It's gonna b ok. He sucks N E Way.*

Since I'm stuck in my room, I turn on my music. Music always makes me feel better. And it's Christmas time. Christmas songs are the best!

The first song that blasts through my iPod speakers is the Chris Brown version of "This Christmas." As soon as I hear, "Hang all the mistletoe . . ." I burst into tears. That was Mario's solo in the glee club Christmas concert.

Next track!

Now, I'm listening to Mariah Carey's sweet voice singing "All I Want for Christmas Is You." This is so obviously an immediate sad face. All I want for Christmas is to go back in time to when Mario was still my boyfriend.

I start to cry again.

I hear a knock on my door. "Go away," I say.

"This isn't Layla. This is mom. I'm coming in."

This is one of those times I wish I had a lock on

my bedroom door. My mother doesn't believe in teenagers having locks. She says that until I pay some bills that I don't deserve privacy. So unfair.

She sits at the end of my bed and gives me her look of sympathy. I must look really busted, because she usually gives me this look when I'm sick with the flu.

"Honey, I want you to get dressed and go somewhere with Cheyenne and Todrick."

"I thought I was on punishment until infinity."

"Well, your dad and I talked about it. We think you're in enough pain, but you're going to make restitution for that go-kart you destroyed with your recklessness. Your father asked them how much it's going to cost to repair it and the owner says two thousand dollars."

"That's a lot of money," I say.

"It is, and you're going to earn every penny of it. Your father is paying them the money so that you aren't banned from their establishment."

"I'll never be able to earn that much money."

"Yes you will. Your father called his friend Herman who owns Good Eatin' Family Restaurant, and you are the new prep cook and waitress."

My eyes just about pop out of my head. Good Eatin' is a hood restaurant that serves delicious food, but it's really, really hood. They've got duct tape on the windows and the place looks like a shack. Still, everyone goes there after church on Sunday for good old-fashioned soul food.

"Mom, I don't know anyone who would work there."

She smiles. "Yes you do. You know yourself!"

"First I break up with Mario, now I have to be embarrassed by a job in the hood? Why don't I just die?"

My mother laughs out loud. "This will be good for you, and it will help you get your mind off of Mario. Why don't you call Cheyenne? You guys can go to the movies or something to celebrate your new job."

My mom gets up and kisses my forehead. This makes me smile. As she leaves, I think about my new job. This does *not* make me smile. This gives me a straight up frowny face.

Even if I do somehow survive being struck by a stray bullet in a drive-by shooting, this will be the death of my social life. Slinging chicken dinners in the hood. Soooo not my style.

But then ramming go-karts into walls while trying to smash ex-boyfriends is not really my style either. Go figure.

And wow . . . I just thought of Mario as my ex-boyfriend.

# 5

---

Cheyenne, Todrick, and I chill out at our favorite table in Applebee's. We decided against the movies, because we have stuff we need to talk about. Namely, me getting over Mario.

"So, Crash and Burn, does Mario need to be afraid? Are you going to run him down with your bike now?" Todrick asks before stuffing a riblet in his mouth.

"Ha, ha. Not funny. I was not trying to run him down. I just wanted to make his go-kart crash into the tires on the side," I explain.

"Like yours did?" Cheyenne asks.

"Yes. I wanted everyone to laugh at him."

"Like everyone laughed at you?" Todrick asks.

"Yeah, pretty much. Thank you both for rubbing it in. You're the bestest friends ever."

Cheyenne smiles at me. "You wouldn't know what to do without us."

I scan the restaurant looking for a sign of Mario. If he steps up in here, we've got to go. And quickly. Everyone hangs out here on the breaks and stuff, because it stays open late, and if you get here before nine, they don't kick you out if you're not over eighteen.

"Two days until Christmas!" Todrick says. "Can't wait to get my stuff."

"Are you still having a Christmas?" Cheyenne asks. "I heard my mom telling my dad that your parents were heated about the go-kart incident."

"I am still having a Christmas, thank you very much. As you can see, I'm not even grounded," I reply.

Todrick asks, "So what's the catch? I know your parents aren't letting you off that easily."

"They feel sorry for me, because I'm so sad about Mario."

Todrick and Cheyenne look at each other, and then back at me. "Spill it," they say in unison.

"Well, it's really not so bad. It's actually kind of cool what I have to do to help pay for the repairs on the go-kart."

"What do you have to do?" Cheyenne asks.

"I just have to get a job. That's all."

Todrick says, "That's not so bad. Do you want me to see if I can get you a job at the rec center with me? We could always use another person on bathroom detail."

I shake my head. "Thanks, but no thanks. My dad already got me a job."

"Cool. Where are you going to be working?" Todrick asks.

"Good Eatin'."

Cheyenne spits a mouthful of soda across the table. "What?"

"I know you've been there, Cheyenne. Stop tripping." I roll my eyes at her and eat a nacho full of skillet queso. Isn't this already bad enough without her tripping?

"You're going to work in that greasy cholesterol factory? Everything they make there has a layer of grease on top of it," Cheyenne says with obvious disgust in her tone.

"Their food is good. That's not what I'm worried about. Have you seen their employees?" Todrick asks. "I don't know how well you'll fit in."

"What are you talking about? I'll be fine." I don't know if I'm convinced of this, but whatever. I'm not going to let them ride me about this.

Todrick says, "The teenagers who work there are kind of . . . rough. Those girls aren't anything like you."

"What exactly are you trying to say Todrick?" I ask.

"Okay, let me break it down for you. You sing in the *Glee Club*! I bet their school doesn't even have a glee club."

Cheyenne laughs. "Okay! Girl, you are too suburban for that crew."

"I'm not listening to y'all! I'm just glad that I don't have to be grounded."

All of a sudden, Cheyenne and Todrick get eerily silent. Since they're both staring at the door, I'm afraid to look.

As our waitress walks by, Cheyenne says, "Can we have our check, please?"

"I'm not done eating!" I say.

Todrick says, "Yeah, you kinda are."

Against my better judgment, I turn my head to look at where Todrick and Cheyenne are looking. I should've known. Of course Mario and Dorie would be here. That's exactly the kind of week I've been having.

They're walking over to a table on the other side of the restaurant. Thank goodness for that. They're with some seniors, too. A perfectly fun looking crew. Dorie hangs all over Mario like she's his Siamese twin or something.

"Ugh," I say. "Gross. How is it that they are already so close? What did I miss? I thought Mario and I were kicking it hard."

"There were signs, Zoey. You just weren't paying attention," Cheyenne says.

"What signs? I was just thinking about this earlier. I had no idea that he was playing me."

"Okay, maybe you didn't know he was playing you, but you should've known that he wasn't feeling you anymore."

I shake my head. "Nope, didn't know."

Todrick asks, "Check your phone. How many texts did you have from him last week?"

I take my phone out and count them. There were seven.

"Seven texts. I don't know what that proves."

Todrick asks, "Did he initiate any of them or are they all responses to you?"

I look at my phone again. Every single last text message that I have from him was in response to something I said first.

"Okay . . . so they are all responses. What does that have to do with anything?"

"It means that all week, he didn't think of you enough to send you a text on his own. When I like a girl, I text her," Todrick says.

"You have girlfriends?" Cheyenne asks. "Who knew? You must introduce me to these unfortunate females."

Todrick shakes his head. "Whatever."

Hello! This is so not about their joking around. This is about me discovering that my ex-boyfriend was cheating on me.

Cheyenne says, "So he didn't text you last week. Did he even call?"

I bring up the call log. I see four calls from my phone to Mario. I remember making all four, because I was irritated that he wasn't calling me right back. Was it because he was talking to Dorie? It didn't occur to me then, but of course, it occurs to me now.

I shake my head. "Nope. Not once."

"See, Zoey. He's been giving you signs. You just haven't paid attention."

"So now what?" I ask. "I'm supposed to go to school every day and see them together? What's that gonna be like? I'm going to ask my mom if I can go to private school or something."

Todrick replies, "You would leave me and Cheyenne because of Mario?"

I wouldn't want to leave them, but just having Dorie and Mario across the restaurant from me is so painful. I can't even begin to imagine seeing them every day, in the hallway, holding hands or on the Glee Club field trips sharing a seat on the bus.

"First of all, Mario and Dorie will not be dating long. Her dating life span is like three weeks tops," Cheyenne says. "He'll probably try to get back with you . . ."

"You think?" I ask.

"Yes, and you're going to say no."

"I am?"

"Yes, because you are going to be on to the next one," Todrick says.

I slide down in my seat so that I can no longer see Mario and Dorie. "I'm done with boys. I don't know when they like me, and I have no idea what to do when I like them. Mario happened completely by accident."

"Aren't there rules?" Todrick asks. "I mean if there were it would be so much easier for everybody."

"There *are* rules," Cheyenne says. "But Zoey only needs to know what *not* to do when she meets a boy that she likes."

55

"Well tell me. Not that I think I'm going to meet another boy that I like . . . but just in case . . ."

"Rule number one. He makes the first move."

Todrick rolls his eyes. "That is so not fair. What if the guy is shy? Sometimes I like to know that I at least have a chance before I holla at a girl."

Cheyenne throws a french fry at him. "Hush, Todrick. You don't talk to girls anyway."

"Okay, I always follow that rule anyway. I never talk to guys first," I say. "What else do you have?"

"Let him request you as a friend on Facebook, not the other way around."

"That doesn't matter at all," Todrick says. "You're just making stuff up."

"It does matter."

"Where are you getting these rules from, Cheyenne?"

She shrugs. "Where else? *Cosmo Girl*!"

Todrick bursts into laughter. "Oh, no wonder this doesn't make any sense. Zoey if you see a guy that you like, you should smile at him and let him know, then if you're friendly, he'll holla . . . unless he has a girlfriend. Because you're pretty and funny."

I give Todrick a blank stare. It feels weird getting a compliment from him. He's like a brother or something—not a boy.

**SO OVER IT**

Cheyenne says, "I cut an article out of the magazine for you to read."

She hands me the cutout piece of paper. "Thanks, I guess. Can we go now? I don't want to be under the same roof with *them* anymore."

As we stand to leave the restaurant, I steal a glance over in Mario's direction. His laughter actually drew my attention. He seems to be having such a great time with Dorie. I don't remember him ever laughing that hard when we were dating.

"Come on," Cheyenne says. "You're staring. Remember? On to the next one, like Todrick said."

I'm not an 'on to the next one' kind of girl. Why don't they understand that? I don't want to move on. I want to be sad for awhile, and then . . . well I don't know what's next. And isn't that okay? I don't want to follow any rules.

Rules are for suckas.

# 6

——

"**O**pen my present now!" my sister Layla squeals.

My mother makes a huge production of opening our gifts. It started when we were little and my dad took us shopping for little pieces of fake jewelry or plants that died a week after we bought them. Layla is always more eager than I am to have her present opened.

My mom smiles and opens Layla's gift. It's a coconut scented bath set from Bath and Body Works. Pretty decent gift. Coconut is our mom's favorite scent and she buys stuff like this all the time.

"Should I open yours now, Zoey?" my mom asks.

"Sure."

My gift is a Terry McMillan book, my mom's favorite author, a new coffee mug, and some herbal tea. I know that I really hooked it up!

"Zoey, this is great! Thank you!"

"You're welcome."

I glance under our tree, and see the two gifts that I had wrapped for Mario. I meant to take those away, but I didn't. I couldn't. It seemed like such a final thing to do.

"Whose are those?" Layla asks. "Are those mine?"

My mom shakes her head. "I think they belong to Zoey."

I feel the serious urge to share a little Christmas cheer and take the gifts over to Mario's house. Would that be so bad? I mean, I bought them for him. I would feel crazy taking them back to the store, plus is there a rule that says I can't be nice to my ex-boyfriend and that we can't be friends? I'm sure that Cheyenne would create one if there isn't.

"What are you thinking about honey?" my mom asks.

"I was thinking . . . that I want to take a walk. Is that okay?" I ask.

"Yeah, sure. Just be back in time for breakfast."

I grab up the two gifts that I got for Mario and walk toward the door. His house is three streets over from ours, but he lives all the way at the other end of his. It's about a ten minute walk, so I've got plenty of time to talk myself out of this venture.

"Zoey. Are you sure you want to do this?" My mom asks.

I should've known I wasn't going to get away without hearing a lecture. "Yes."

"I know that you bought those gifts for Mario, but honey, it's kind of desperate."

I look at the floor and let out a big sigh. It is desperate. I just want to have a face to face conversation with him. I need to see his face when he says that he doesn't want to be my boyfriend anymore.

One of the gifts falls from my hand to the floor. I can't go over to his house. What if Dorie is over there? Unlikely, but possible.

"Thanks for my presents, mom and dad," I say with a quivering voice. "I'm going upstairs now. I'll be down for dinner."

My dad says, "No, Zoey. You're not going to go into your room and cry the day away. You're going to spend it with your family. Today is a holiday."

Why won't they just let me go into my hideout to cry? I don't want to do this in front of them. My dad pretends not to look at me when he puts a DVD in the player.

"Who's up for some *Despicable Me*?" my dad asks.

Watching movies all day on Christmas, while we're waiting on dinner, is our family tradition.

Layla says, "Me, daddy! I want to watch it!"

I roll my eyes and give a little headshake. Layla

takes this Daddy's Little Girl routine way too far
sometimes. Usually, it doesn't bother me, but
today I'm not in the mood.

As soon as my dad turns off the lights in the
family room, I let my tears fall. Every time I think
that I'm done crying, it starts all over again. Sitting
here watching this stupid movie with my dad and
little sister is not helping.

I thought that I was going to be with Mario forever. I know that's kind of crazy since we're only
seventeen, and hardly anybody ever stays with
their first boyfriend for the rest of their life, but I
thought we'd be the exception.

Since I can't pay attention to the movie, I think
about our first dance. Mario took me to the
Spring Fling, and we dressed alike. We both wore
white T-shirts, jeans, and black and white Chucks.
Very simple, but everyone could tell we were together when we walked in.

I remember wanting to dance. Mario had said,
"I don't really dance all that well, but I'll try if you
want me to."

"You can't dance?"

"Um . . . no. You think that just because I'm a
blatino that I can dance?"

I had laughed out loud at Mario's word that
he'd created. Blatino. His mother is Puerto Rican
and his father is black. He's biracial and bilingual.
I remember thinking that him being able to speak
fluent Spanish was hot.

Apparently, I'm not the only one who thinks

Nikki Carter

that he's hot. Dorie sure had no problem snatching him up. I am surprised that she likes him, though. He's not incredibly popular like all of her past boyfriends.

My mom calls from the kitchen. "Someone's at the door. Go answer it!"

Since daddy and Layla are wrapped up in their stupid movie, I get up to get it. It better not be Christmas carolers. I am soooo not in the mood.

I throw the front door open, ready to dismiss whoever's there, and guess what? It is someone in total need of dismissing—Mario.

"What do you want?" I ask.

He holds out a box. "I'd bought you this for Christmas, so my mom told me to bring it over."

I look down at the box, but I don't take it. "Why don't you just give it to your new girlfriend?"

"Have you been crying?" he asks.

"No. Allergies."

"Oh, well. I was just bringing this. My mom is waiting in the car. We're going to my grandmother's house. Are you going to take it?"

I take the box from him and consider giving him the gifts that I have under the tree. "Hold on a second."

I run to retrieve the two packages from under our tree. My mom just stares at me with a hopeful look on her face, but she doesn't say anything.

"Here," I say when I get back to the door. "I got you stuff, too."

He swallows hard and looks at me. "Um . . . Zoey . . . I'm sorry for breaking up with you on Facebook. My mom says it was cowardly. It's just that . . . well . . . I liked Dorie before you and I got together."

"Listen. Don't keep explaining. Sorry is enough."

I don't want to hear how much he was in love with Dorie before we met, and how he just *had* to break up with me because she finally paid him some attention. That is not helping at all.

"Okay. We can still be cool, right?"

I give him my confused face. How are we cool? I just had what will probably go down as the most embarrassing moment of my life all because of him. Not feeling any motivation for coolness here. It actually annoys me that he asks this, like I'm some kind of idiot.

"I'll see you around, I'm sure. Glee club and stuff. You know."

He nods. "Okay, then. Merry Christmas."

Mario trots back to his mother's car, and I can see her smiling. I guess she made him do the big boy thing and face his ex-girlfriend. Maybe she's even proud of him. Okay, then. Whatever.

I close the door and walk back to the family room to finish the stupid movie with my dad and sister. I am glad that I didn't go to his house to take him those presents. Glad I listened to my mom on that.

Somehow, I thought seeing Mario again would make me feel better. Kind of thought he might take one look at me and realize that he made a mistake, and that of course he should be my boyfriend. But hearing his lame excuse doesn't make me feel better at all.

I sit down in the armchair that I'd claimed earlier and open the package. Inside are two Aeropostale T-shirts. That I already own. Wow. He didn't even pay enough attention to me to know which shirts I rock on the regular? This makes me sad.

But it also wakes me all the way up. Mario was just not that into me.

Big sigh.

# 7

I really don't know why I have to start this job thing during winter break. I mean, I know Christmas is over and everything, but I'd really like to enjoy the rest of my vacation before I start getting fried chicken smell all over me.

My dad drops me off here at seven o'clock in the morning. A completely ridiculous time to have to be awake during my break. Why couldn't I do the afternoon or evening shift? I have to be here at the crack of dawn.

But since my dad reminded me that me having to work here is all my fault because of my "horse-play" at GoKart Heaven, I really don't have a leg to stand on. It's funny, I think my mom is the only one who realizes that I was trying to crash into Mario's go-kart. Everyone else just fusses at me for not driving the thing safely.

As soon as I step in the door, there's a teenage girl waiting. She's wearing some really, really tight Apple Bottoms jeans and a tiny Aeropostale T-shirt. I didn't know girls in the hood liked Aeropostale!

"Are you Zoey?" she asks.

"Yes."

"I'm Kellita. Follow me."

She leads me to a big kitchen with stainless steel appliances. The kitchen is actually bigger than the rest of the restaurant, which only had a counter space to wait for your food, a couple of tables and chairs, and a pop machine. It's not really a dine-in establishment. You pick up your food and then you take it home to enjoy.

In the kitchen, there's a boy about my age, chopping a pile of vegetables. He looks up at me and nods, then goes back to his work. He's kind of cute. Dark brown skin, low fade, rhinestone stud in his ear. Hood, but cute.

"That's Kellin, my twin brother."

"So, tell me why I have to be here this early," I say.

A loud booming voice comes from behind me. "Because this is when the real work gets done."

I turn around and find myself standing face to face with the meanest looking woman I've ever seen up close. Her face has folds of fat on the cheeks and chin, and her eyes seem to be swallowed up in the lumpiness. Like two little raisins pressed into brown bread dough. I swallow hard and wish I could make myself disappear.

"I'm Mrs. Owens. Here is your apron. Kellita will show you the ropes. I hope you last longer than the last girl I had. She was disappointing."

Mrs. Owens turns and stomps out of the kitchen. With every step, each of her massive butt cheeks jiggles and shakes. It's like a booty earthquake or something.

I shudder at the thought of my behind ever looking like that. Then, I chuckle. Hopefully, when I see Dorie at our twenty year reunion her badonkadonk looks just like Mrs. Owens's badonka-DANG!

Kellita hands me a hair net. "Put this over your weave."

"I don't have a weave!" I say, my hand subconsciously going to my long straight locks.

"You are kinda bright yellow. Are you mixed?"

"Like biracial? No. I'm just black," I reply.

"For real? Them light cat eyes and all that hair and you're just black?"

I shrug. "As far as I know."

Kellita walks over to the giant sink and motions for me to follow her. "Wash your hands for sixty seconds. Count to sixty while you do it. Mama likes her kitchen clean."

"Have you ever done prep cooking before?" Kellita asks.

I shrug. "I don't think so."

"Have you done *any* cooking before? What do you know how to prepare?"

I think for a moment. "Well, I know how to

make scrambled eggs, pancakes, bacon, and macaroni and cheese."

"Hmmm . . ." Kellita says. "Let's try you out on the macaroni detail then."

"No wait, let me explain. When I say macaroni and cheese, I mean out of the blue box. I don't know how to make Good Eatin' macaroni and cheese."

Which . . . let me say . . . is some of the best macaroni and cheese on the planet. That's probably how Mrs. Owens's booty got that big—grubbing on that macaroni and cheese.

Kellin looks up from his pile of onions and says, "Just give her a knife and the celery. Don't put her on no macaroni and cheese on the first day. You trying to get rid of another one?"

Kellita snickers and hands me a knife and points at the pile of celery. "Chop those up into little pieces."

I guess I look confused, because she asks, "You don't know how to chop celery?"

"Can you just demonstrate one? I'm sure I can do it, I just want to do it right."

Kellita sighs and takes the knife from my hand. Swiftly and effortlessly, she chops up the celery stalk. In like fifteen seconds flat, the once whole stalk is now in tiny symmetrical pieces.

"There you go," Kellita says. "You try."

I bite my bottom lip as I attempt to chop the celery like Kellita. I am much clumsier, it takes me longer, and my pieces are nowhere near symmetrical.

Kellita shakes her head. "Just keep practicing. I'm going up front to bundle money."

I hear Kellita chuckle under her breath as she leaves the kitchen. I want to go up front and count money! I'm much better at that than chopping celery. This is not what I had in mind.

"Do we have to stay back here all day, chopping stuff?" I ask Kellin.

He shakes his head. "No. After we finish the prep work, Mama Owens comes in. Then she wants us out of the way. She's the chef and she's got one assistant."

"So the prep stuff is just chopping vegetables?"

"No. We have to make the cornbread for the dressing, boil the eggs for the potato salad and take off the shells, and clean the chicken."

"That sounds like a lot. How long do we have?"

"Two hours. Kellita will come back and help. She's preheating all of the ovens now. That's for the cornbread."

I start chopping another piece of celery, because obviously, it's not going to chop itself. I don't want to do this, but I don't see them giving me any other job. At least I don't have to chop the onions. My eyes are watering and I'm at the other end of the table.

"It doesn't bother you to cut the onions?" I ask.

"No. It doesn't burn me."

"Wow, you're special. Most people can't stand chopping onions."

He shrugs. "Sometimes when Kellita does it she uses the vegetable chopper. Mama Owens doesn't like that though, because it mashes the vegetable. She wants us to do it the old-fashioned way."

"So where do you go to school?" I ask. "I go to Lewisville High."

"Skyline," he replies. "Oak Cliff."

"You play any sports?"

"Football. And I work here. That's it," Kellin says.

He definitely looks like he plays football. He's built like an athlete.

Kellita pokes her head through the kitchen door. "Kellin, your little girlfriend is out here. You need to check her before I get at her. For real."

Kellin sighs. "Man, Lita! Tell her I'm working."

"Uh-uh, nope. You need to deal with this chick. She is getting on my nerves. And you know Mama Owens is fixing to cuss her out."

Kellin snatches off his apron and wipes his hands on some paper towels. "I'll be right back Zoey," he says.

I'm curious to see what Kellin's girlfriend looks like, but I don't dare peep out of that door. Not with Kellita and Mama Owens waiting to pounce on me for doing something wrong. What would make a girl come up to her boyfriend's job early in the morning? Sounds like drama to me.

"Kellin, I know you were creeping with her! My girl saw you with her at the mall. Stop playing!" The girlfriend is *loud*. So loud that I can hear her through the big double metal doors.

Kellin yells, "Stop tripping Desiree! We don't even go together anymore, so how am I creeping?"

The alleged girlfriend, apparently named Desiree says, "We don't go together? Since when, Kellin? We just went out the other night, but we're not together?"

"That was a group of people! Ooh! Can you just leave?"

Kellin bursts back through the kitchen doors and I pretend to be cutting celery. He goes back to his chopping, and it's like he's trying to murder those poor vegetables.

I shake my head and give him some serious side eye. Just another cheating boyfriend. Are all guys like this? Do they all just think they can play games with us and move on to the next girl?

After chopping in silence for awhile, Kellin says, "Do you need any help on that celery?"

"Yeah, I guess."

Kellin comes and stands next to me. He wipes his knife down with a cloth and starts chopping.

"Can I ask you a question?" I say.

"Yeah, what's up?"

"Why does your girlfriend think you're still together if you say that y'all aren't?"

"You heard that?"

"I think the entire street heard it. Y'all were pretty loud."

Kellin sighs and sticks his knife in the cutting board. "Sorry about that. Desiree was tripping anyway."

"Clearly she thinks that y'all still have something. Why would she be up here tripping if she didn't? Boys are so ignorant . . ."

"Wait a minute," Kellin says. "You don't know what went down between me and Desiree. Maybe you should ask before you make an opinion of me."

I roll my eyes and keep cutting the celery. As if I need to hear his explanation! He probably told her he wasn't feeling her anymore, after he started kicking it with someone else. Boys are all the same. Why should this guy be any different?

Kellita comes back into the kitchen cracking up laughing. "Mama Owens said that if that girl come back up through here, she's gonna cut her. And you know she ain't playing."

Kellin grumbles something under his breath and goes back over to his pile of onions. He starts scraping them into a huge metal container which he then sits next to the range top.

"I don't suppose you've ever attempted cornbread," Kellita asks me.

"Do Jiffy corn muffins count?"

Kellita huffs out loud. "Oh, my goodness! Why did they hire you? I've been trying to get my girl a job up here for months and she can cook her butt off. Then, out of the blue, they hire your old non-cooking self."

"Why does she have to cook anyway?" Kellin asks. "She can take orders. Then, she won't have to be back here with me since she thinks I'm so ignorant."

Kellita cracks up laughing. "Well, Zoey, we've got one thing in common. We both think Kellin is ignorant."

"Man, forget both of y'all, and Desiree's hood-rat self."

"Whatever, Kellin," Kellita says. "You just gonna have to get used to people thinking you're ignorant, because there's no way I'm giving up my post on the register to cut onions. Come on, Zoey. Let me show you how to make this cornbread. It's easy. You'll be making it by yourself soon."

I watch Kellita carefully as she mixes a whole bag of self-rising corn meal mix with buttermilk, eggs, and oil. After she's done mixing she sets the bowl to the side.

"It's good to let cornbread rest a little bit before you bake it. It rises better. Oh, and make sure when you start in the morning to take out the eggs and buttermilk and set them on the counter. Then, they can be room temperature when we finally get to mixing the batter."

"How many pans do we have to make?" I ask.

"We have to make ten big pans in the morning. On Sundays we make more because everybody comes here for Sunday dinner after church."

I nod. "I know. We come here all the time."

"Well, I promise you, after cooking and eating this stuff every day, you won't want to look at another plate full of macaroni and cheese, greens or candied yams. I never eat this stuff anymore."

"I don't think I can ever get sick of soul food. I love it!" I say. "And my mom doesn't do much cooking because she works a lot."

Kellita seems interested. "What does your mother do?"

"She's a disaster recovery manager at a bank. So sometimes she has to be gone days at a time."

"What does a disaster recovery manager even do? Does she fix computers or something like that? Did she go to school for that?"

"Yes, she went to school for it. She has a bachelor's degree in Computer Science."

"I wonder if I can get that at the community college," Kellita says. "It sounds like your mother has a good job."

"Well, it's a four year degree, but you could go to the University of Texas or the University of North Texas. They both have that degree, I'm sure."

Kellin sucks his teeth. "She is not taking both of her kids to a college like that. She's gonna end up working here at the restaurant."

"And what are you gonna do if you don't get a football scholarship?" she asks. "You're gonna be right here with me cutting onions and making cornbread."

"Well, what's wrong with working for the family business?" I ask. "I guess I don't see anything wrong with that."

Kellin replies, "That's because this is your first day. Work here a week, or a month, and you'll know why we hate it."

"Yeah," Kellita says. "Every day before school we have to come here and chop vegetables before we go to school. Kellin goes to school smelling like an onion all the time."

"It's hard to wash off. Eventually, by the end of the day, I'm straight, but then I have to come right back here and wait tables. Then, I try to get a jump on some of the prep cooking for the next day. It sucks," Kellin says.

"Except during football season! He gets a pass," Kellita says. "No one makes him do anything during the football season. They're all hoping that he goes to the NFL and that no one will have to work anymore."

"Who keeps your kids during the day?" I ask Kellita.

"My mother. She's got our baby brother at home. He's got special needs, so she's gotta take care of him all day. She just keeps mine too."

In this moment, I am so glad to have my life. I wouldn't want to have to worry about being a mother, working, and having to choose community college if that's not what I wanted.

Compared to what Kellita has to deal with, this stuff with Mario is just a little bit unimportant.

"Now, we put the cornbread in the ovens. It takes each pan about thirty minutes to bake."

76 "But the back of the package says twenty to twenty-five minutes."

Kellita shakes her head. "Girl, will you listen to me and stop being a know-it-all? These ovens, for some reason, cook a tad bit slower than average, so we cook longer. If you want to see Mama Owens flip out, give her some half cooked cornbread."

"Or some burned cornbread," Kellin adds.

"She'd rather it be burned than undercooked. She can work with the burned."

"This is too complicated," I say. "I'm afraid I'm going to mess something up."

"Don't worry," Kellita says. "At first, I was gonna set you up to fail, but I actually kind of dig you. I thought you'd be stuck up, but you're not."

My jaw drops. "Why would you think that?"

"Because you live in Lewisville."

"Wow, you were just gonna judge me on my neighborhood?" I ask indignantly.

"Yeah. Most black girls from over there are up-pity," Kellita says.

Kellin interjects, "You can't talk, Zoey. You judged me based on a conversation you over-heard. Said I was ignorant based on Desiree act-ing a fool."

"He's ignorant," Kellita says, "but not because of Desiree. Desiree played him."

My eyes widen. "For real?"

Kellita replies, "Yep. She messed with some other guy on the football team and got pregnant by him, then tried to blame it on Kellin."

"She's pregnant?" I ask. "Wow . . . how do you know it's not yours Kellin?"

Kellin leaves the table and struts over to me and Kellita near the ovens. "Somebody is all up in my mix."

He smiles at me and I'm shocked at how attractive he is when he smiles. He's incredibly cute.

"So how do you know?" I ask. "Inquiring minds want to know!"

"Because I know how to do simple math. The dates didn't add up."

Kellita says, "Yeah, he broke up with her in July. It's Christmas and she's three months pregnant."

I burst into laughter. "She thought you'd fall for that?"

"You think it's funny, but I think she's convinced herself that it's true," Kellin says. "You heard her. She's still trying to pretend like I'm gonna be her baby's father, and her man."

"That's kind of crazy," I say.

"That's a whole lotta crazy," Kellita says. "But if she keeps messing with Mama Owens, it's gonna be curtains."

The twins crack up laughing together and for the first time, I can see their resemblance. Their body types are nothing alike. She's short and curvy, probably how Mama Owens was when she was seventeen.

Mama Owens bursts through the doors with her assistant, a ridiculously skinny black dude who looks as if he could use an entire vat of lotion. I've never seen anyone so ashy. It's like he jumped out of the shower, dried off, and ran through a gigantic flour sifter.

"With all this laughing going on in here, I can't believe anyone's getting any work done. Have y'all started on the chicken?"

Kellita says, "Kellin and I cleaned it last night. It's in the refrigerator."

"Humph. I wanted Zoey to learn how to clean chicken."

Kellita says, "We'll teach her tomorrow. Do you think I could get off early today, Mama Owens?"

"Get off early? For what?" she asks.

"It's warm outside and I want to take the babies to the zoo. They would like that."

Mama Owens rolls her eyes. "Them babies is too little to care anything about the zoo. They just two years old! All they care about is sipping them dang sippy cups all day."

"Mama Owens . . . please!"

"Who's gonna run the register if I let you go early?"

"Me! Me!" Mama Owens' ashy assistant is just a little bit too eager.

Mama Owens replies, "Lester, you know good and well you ain't running no register."

"I'll do it," Kellin says. "And I'll teach Zoey too, so Kellita can have a backup."

"All right then," Mama Owens says. "But this is your last time this week. Don't ask again."

Kellin and I go to the front of the restaurant. "So, I'm gonna teach you how to open the restaurant, but . . ."

"But what?" I ask.

"Are you sure you're going to be able to learn anything from me? Being that I'm so ignorant and all."

"That was my bad, Kellin. I jumped to conclusions."

"As long as you don't let *that* happen again, we might end up being friends."

Friends with a handsome, athletic football player from Skyline High School? Hmmm . . . not typical Zoey, but I think it just might work.

# 8

"So what was your first day like as a member of working class America?" Todrick asks as we chill at Main Event.

"It sucked!" I say.

We're watching a group of kids from our high school bowl. It's a bowling party, I guess, but only a handful of people are bowling. The rest, like us, are sitting at tables behind the lanes.

I didn't really feel like coming because my feet hurt like heck. Standing up all day, taking and filling orders was too much. I've never worked that hard in my life. There were servers who put the food in the take-out containers, but I had to check it, bag it, and hand it to the customer. If Kellin hadn't been there helping me, I don't know how I would've survived.

Cheyenne says, "Did you meet anyone interesting? Any cute guys? Seems like I remember one working there."

"I met these twins, Kellin and Kellita. They go to Skyline . . ."

"Hood alert!" Todrick says. "Hood alert!"

"Stop it! They're really cool. Their grand-mother runs the kitchen."

Cheyenne puts one finger in the air. "Wait. Kellin Owens? Quarterback of the Skyline High Raiders?"

"Oh, he didn't mention he was the quarter-back. You know I don't follow sports," I reply.

"Yeah, he went All American his sophomore year and his junior year. They think he's going to get a full ride somewhere, and probably go pro before he graduates from college."

"Wow. He didn't mention any of this," I say.

It's crazy that Kellin didn't tell me any of these great things about himself. Just the fact that he's still working in his family restaurant is tripped out. I'm sure if he threw his weight around a little, no one would make him chop onions or clean the fat out of chicken thighs (yeah, you don't even want to know. Grosser than gross).

"I bet he's a jerk," Todrick says. "Most QB-1's are jerks."

"Actually, he was really cool," I say. "He showed me the ropes. How to cut celery and clean chicken."

Cheyenne makes a gagging noise. "You had to

clean chicken? See this is what I'm talking about. If you have to clean a piece of meat, why would you then go and put that in your body? That's disgusting."

"Stop being such a vegan," Todrick says.

"I'm not a vegan. I am a vegetarian. There's a difference."

"Do either of them eat hot dogs?" Todrick asks.

"Ew!! No. Unless they're tofu dogs."

I tune out of Cheyenne and Todrick's pointless argument about nothing. I think about Kellin and that girl trying to pin a baby on him. He better be careful. He could end up with a child support order before he graduates.

"So . . . did he ask you for your number?" Cheyenne asks.

I scrunch my eyebrows into a frown. "Who? Kellin? No. It's not like that. We're cool, that's all."

"Why is that all? Does he have a girlfriend?" Cheyenne asks.

"Don't know. Didn't ask," I reply.

Todrick says, "I thought you were moving on to the next one. If this guy is available, he might be a good one."

Why are my two friends ready to pass me off to the next boy like I'm some kind of old maid, living with my parents at the age of fifty, and starting a collection of cats and house dresses? I'm seventeen and I just broke up with my boyfriend last week! Is there something that says I have to replace him within seven days or less? If there is no one gave me that memo. I'm tired of missing memos of such crucial relevance! Blank stare.

"I'm not ready for another boyfriend yet. I'm still kind of on Mario."

Cheyenne slams her hand down on the table. "How are you still on him? I thought we had moved beyond that."

"Not on him as in trying to get back with him. I just am not ready for a new dude."

"Why the heck not?" Cheyenne asks. "There's nothing like a new boo, to help you get over an ex-boo."

"Where do you come up with this stuff?" I ask.

*"Cosmo Girl."*

I lift an eyebrow. "Well, what does *Cosmo Girl* say about you when your ex-boyfriend brings you a Christmas present on Christmas Day?"

Cheyenne's eyes widen. "Mario brought you a present?"

"Yeah, some Aeropostale T-shirts that I already had."

Cheyenne frowns and shakes her head. "I can't stand him. He couldn't be more original than that?"

"I didn't care. I gave them to Layla. It's whatever."

Todrick asks, "You didn't give him that crunk Hollister T-shirt and Fossil watch did you?"

"Yeah, I gave it to him. I shouldn't have. I should've taken it back to the store and used the money for that stupid go-kart. Do y'all know that's gonna cost two thousand dollars to fix?"

"Word?" Todrick asks.

"Word! That's why I'm stuck chopping celery every morning for the rest of the break."

"Are you gonna work there when we go back to school?" Cheyenne asks. "If so, this could be problematic."

"I'm going to work there on Wednesday nights from five until nine o'clock, Friday from five until nine, and Saturday from noon until eight."

"That's pretty much your whole weekend!" Todrick says.

"It's not the whole weekend. I've got after nine on Friday. Late night skate doesn't even start until nine thirty. And we'll still have time to get into Applebee's on Saturday."

"Not liking working class America," Todrick says. "You're messing up our trio."

"Why don't you get a girlfriend? Then you'll have something to do," Cheyenne teases.

"When are you going to get a boyfriend? You're always on me, and dissing Zoey about her break ups!"

Oh, for crying out loud! I wish these two would stop fronting and just get together.

"When I want a boyfriend, I'll have one. The guys are lining up!"

I shake my head. "I'll be back. I have to go to the bathroom."

"TMI!" Todrick says in his frantically-pitched voice.

Hopefully, they're done with their pretend spat by the time I get back to the table.

The bathroom is disgusting, as usual. What is it about teenagers storming a place and destroying the bathroom facilities? I get a big wad of toilet paper and start wiping stuff down inside the last stall (which is hopefully the least used).

I hear voices outside the stall. Annoying voices. Mindy and Ashley, Dorie's cheerleader friends. They are the last people I'm trying to see right now.

"He's just a glee club geek. It's all a joke, you know," Ashley says.

"I thought it was a joke, but Dorie seems like she really likes him, so I wasn't sure anymore," Mindy replies.

Ashley says, "Dorie's good! She and Ethan both have to date a geek. The one who gets broken up with first loses."

"That is crazy. What's the prize?"

Ashley giggles. "I don't know if there is a prize! I think they just want to do it because they're bored."

Okay, this calls for me holding my pee.

I open the stall door and say, "Dorie stole my boyfriend over a joke?"

"Look, Ash, it's Crash and Burn! How do you like working in the hood?" Mindy asks.

"Whatever. You can tell Dorie that I'm telling

Mario. I'm telling him, so she's going to lose the game."

"You're such a lame," Ashley says. "You should be happy. Dorie showed you Mario's true colors. You would've never known he was a player if it wasn't for her."

I go back into the stall and slam the door. It probably would've been much more dramatic if I'd stormed out of the bathroom angrily. But I really have to pee, and I am not trying to add pee-pee girl to my brand new nickname of Crash and Burn.

I hear Ashley and Mindy leave finally, so then I come back out of the stall. I had to wait for them to leave, because they couldn't see my face. I didn't want them to see me crying about Mario.

I don't want to see me crying. But as I look in the dirty, greasy mirror, the tears are kind of hard to ignore.

# 9

—————

"So what if I do like Cheyenne? Should I tell her? Do you think she'll dog me?" Todrick asks me.

Todrick is sitting with me at our kitchen table. It seems that when I called them out at Main Event that I was on to something. I was just blurting, and now he wants to tell me all about his secret crush. I'm not in the mood, but at least listening to him rant and rave helps me keep my mind off of Mario and Dorie.

"Well, we know that Cheyenne has her rules, right? So you probably should get a *Cosmo Girl* to see how to approach her."

"Funny, funny, ha, ha. I'm not reading any teen girl magazine to tell me how to get a girlfriend. I'm just gonna go for it."

"Have you had a girlfriend before Cheyenne? If

so, please do tell, because I don't recall hearing about it, and we've been friends since the third grade."

"Don't be a hater all your life, Zoey. I've had girlfriends. Remember Madison?"

"Oh . . . how could I forget Madison? But was she your girlfriend, or did she just make you buy her stuff? I don't remember her ever saying that she was officially your girlfriend."

"Well, she sure kissed like my girlfriend."

"Ew . . . did not need to have that visual. At all. No thank you for that."

"So anyway, back to Cheyenne. Should I just say, 'Look, you da best, and I've had you on my radar for like two years now. So, let's both stop fooling ourselves and do the dang thang.'"

I roll my eyes. Hard.

"You are a goofball, Todrick. Don't use any song lyrics in your approach. I'm one hundred percent sure that she won't like that."

"I like song lyrics. They can sometimes say what we're too afraid to put into words."

"I think you should just be like, 'Cheyenne, I think you're a great friend, and I'm crushing on you. Is that okay? Are you crushing on me too?'"

Todrick shakes his head. "No way! That leaves me way too open to embarrassment. That just sounds like I'm begging for her to say, 'Get out of my face.'"

"I know Cheyenne. She will like that you put

yourself on the line like that, and that you aren't afraid to say how you feel. Trust me. I know my girl."

"So you think that will work? Me sounding like a sucka?"

"I don't think that makes you sound like a sucka. Why do guys have to be so hard all the time? Why can't you just be honest? If Mario had just been honest with me, we wouldn't have had such a tripped out situation."

Todrick laughs. "I was wondering when this conversation was going to turn and be about you and Mario again. It actually took longer than I thought it would!"

"Shut up! I was just using that as an example."

"Have you decided what to do about Dorie's game?" Todrick asks. "Are you going to tell him, or let him get played?"

"Part of me wants to tell him, you know? Part of me thinks that maybe once he sees how horrible Dorie is, he'll want us to get back together."

"Do you want that? You want to get back together with him?"

"No. I don't. I just want to feel like I won, you know? If he wants me back and I don't take him, then I've won. Because right now, every time I see him I feel like a big fat loser."

"You're not a loser. You're a girl that got played by a stupid boy."

I nod in agreement. I know, deep down that I

didn't do anything wrong, and that he's the one who's stupid. But really, truly, does any of that matter? I'm the one with the egg on my face.

I'd like to be there to see Mario with egg on *his* face.

# 10

Cleaning chicken is a very disgusting job. You take the chicken thigh or breast and dig down into the crevices to clean out all of the little organs. Envisioning a chicken having kidneys and a liver is pretty disgusting. Having these little things slip between your fingers into a sink is beyond disgusting.

"You're quiet tonight," Kellin says. "It's gonna be pretty boring if we clean all three hundred pieces of chicken in silence."

"How'd we get stuck on chicken duty, tonight? It's Friday! Where's Kellita?"

"She's got a date."

"Wow! I'm here slinging chicken parts and that heifer is on a date?" I throw my hand into the air and a piece of chicken fat flies into my face.

Kellin cracks up and hands me an anti-bacterial wipe. "It's the father of her twin daughters. They're back together for now, and my mother hopes he's gonna marry her."

"Married at seventeen? That's crazy."

He shrugs. "Raising two kids alone at seventeen is crazy."

"Yeah, I guess you're right."

"So what's up with you? Why don't you tell me what's bothering you."

"Why? You don't know me all like that to get in my business."

Kellin chuckles. "You know all about my drama with Desiree. Why don't you want me to know what's up with you?"

"Because you didn't tell me all about you. We worked together all day for two days and you didn't say anything about being the QB-1 at Skyline, nor did you tell me you were an All American."

"Oh. Is that important to you? You a college scout or something?" Kellin asks.

He's got this twinkle thing that happens with his eyes when he's getting smart. It would be really hot if he wasn't getting smart while he was doing it.

"No, but I'd like to know who I'm talking to or making friends with."

"Well football is not who I am. It's one of the things that I do." I would swear that he dropped his voice an octave. Is he doing this on purpose?

"Well, who are you then?"

"I'm Kellin Owens, a funny and smart dude who likes to cook and play sports."

I laugh out loud. "Who told you that you were funny?"

"You're laughing aren't you?"

I take another chicken thigh in my hand and slide the little guts out. After fifty chicken thighs, this is still gross. "Yeah, you are kind of funny."

"Thank you. So tell me about you. Who are you?"

"I'm a singer. I love music, every genre."

"Even heavy metal?"

"Even heavy metal," I say. "Of course I don't like all of the songs in that genre, but there are a few that I like."

"Are you popular in your school?" he asks.

"Nah, not really. I'm not unpopular, but I'm in glee club. I think I probably lose cool points for being in the glee club."

Now he's the one laughing. "Glee club is cool."

"Then why are you laughing?"

"Because I was looking at your face, and thinking you might be cute if you didn't have that hairnet on. Then I remembered the glob of chicken fat that was on your face a minute ago and got grossed out."

"I *might* be cute? Wow. Whatever dude."

"So now that you know me, will you tell me why you've been moping around all evening?"

"My boyfriend and I broke up. Right before Christmas."

Kellin draws in a sharp breath. "Ouch. I'm guessing that you didn't initiate it. Am I right?"

"Yeah. He broke up with me, for another girl . . . a cheerleader."

"Those cheerleaders, man. They're pretty irresistible."

"Do you want me to tell you or not?"

He nods. "Yes, I'm sorry. Please tell me."

"Well . . . I found out that she doesn't really like him. It's all some bet that she has with her real boyfriend. Each of them dates a geek. Whoever gets broken up with first loses."

"Man, y'all suburban kids ain't got nothing better to do, huh? That's just stupid, you know that right?"

"I'm not participating in the game! I am an innocent bystander of the game! I am a victim of the game. I think it's stupid too."

"All of y'all need jobs, just to keep y'all from dreaming up stupid stuff to do." Kellin takes out two long foil pans and begins to load in the cleaned chicken.

"Do you think I should tell my ex-boyfriend that the cheerleader doesn't really like him?"

Kellin places one pan of chicken on the counter and starts filling another. "Why would you tell him? Did he tell you when he started talking to the cheerleader? Did he tell you the exact moment he decided to get with her?"

"No . . ."

"Then you don't owe him anything. Let him figure out on his own that his cheerleader isn't really digging him."

"Well, I don't want to do it because I feel like I owe him something. I don't think that's my reason at all."

Kellin taps his chin as if he's thinking. Then he says, "Oh, I get it. You just want to tell him so you can rub it in. Wow."

"Is that bad? Me wanting to rub it in? He's been mean to me."

"Well, my pastor always says that vengeance belongs to God and not man. Maybe you telling him this is something like revenge."

"Why do you think that?"

"Because I can tell that you don't want him back."

I shake my head. "No. You're right about that. I absolutely don't want him back."

"So you don't need to be the one to say anything."

I chuckle a little bit. "How are you so wise? It's like talking to a guru or something."

"I'm not wise at all. I have no idea how to get rid of a bug-a-boo."

"Who, Desiree?"

"Yep. Desiree."

"Well why can't you get rid of her? I mean . . . she knows that you can't be the father of her baby. I don't see what's so complex about that."

"Can you keep a secret? This one I can't hold in anymore."

I feel a little twinge of excitement. He wants to share his secret with me? Cheyenne would say that this is Kellin trying to holla at me.

"I'm great at keeping secrets."

"There's a chance that Desiree's baby is mine."

I drop my butter knife on the table out of shock. This is the secret he wants to share with me? That he's maybe got a girl pregnant? What would *Cosmo Girl* have to say about this?

"So you hooked up with her after July?"

"Yes, but only once. So, it's slim, but there's still a chance."

I nod slowly, gaining understanding. "So this is why Desiree comes up here acting like a fool? She thinks you're her baby's father."

"I could be."

"What will you do if you are?"

He shrugs. "I'm sure everyone, including Desiree, would want me to still play football and go to college. Because if I go to the NFL, I'll really be able to provide for a baby."

"That would suck though. For you and for the baby. Everyone else would be cool, except for the two of you."

"Yeah that would really suck."

"I hope it's not yours."

"Me too."

"But you won't know until it gets here."

"Nope."

All thoughts of flirting and crushes go out of my mind. Kellin's got real stuff to deal with, potentially being a long-distance father. And the worst thing I can think of is Mario getting played by Dorie.

At the end of the day, all of that is irrelevant. Again, Kellin's life has taught me a lesson about my life . . . in five years nobody's going to remember Crash and Burn and whether I ever kissed Mario behind the bleachers.

I just have to get through the next two weeks.

# 11

——

"I don't really want to go to this party, Cheyenne. I know it's the New Year and all, but I have no desire to party with anyone from Lewisville High School. Plus, it's cold."

Cheyenne ignores me and continues taking out clothes. She looks good. She's got on a silver shimmery sequined top, black leggings, and boots. There's a big silver flower in her gigantic hair, and hoop earrings in her ears. She never puts on makeup. She doesn't have to, because her skin is so pretty. The freckles that pepper the bridge of her nose almost look like beauty marks.

"You're going to this party because everyone needs to know that you are straight. And you are. You're not thinking about Mario's stupid self, nor Dorie's little game. And you've got a new boo at your new job . . ."

"Halt! What the heck are you talking about? I don't have a new boo! If I do, no one told me about him."

"Girl, stop playing! You know I mean Kellin. He's coming to the party, right?"

I shake my head with confusion. "Kellin is not my new boo. He is a new friend."

"Why is he not a new boo. Does he have a girlfriend?"

I think about Desiree. "Um . . . it's kind of complicated. I guess that's the best way to put it."

"But he is coming to the party, though. Even if he's not your new boo, everyone will think that he is."

"I invited Kellin and his sister Kellita. They're twins."

Cheyenne asks, "She's the hood chick that works the register, right?"

"Yep."

"The one with the tattoo of the flower on her chest."

I nod. "That's her. Do you have a problem with me inviting her?"

Cheyenne shakes her head. "I'm just interested to see what happens. This is a social experiment if you will. I love social experiments."

"You suck, Cheyenne! This is not a social experiment. This is me inviting my new friends to a stupid party that I don't really want to go to, but I'm being forced to attend, by my overly pushy best friend."

"Simmer down! You always start spitting run on paragraphs when you get stressed. Dial it back a little bit mama. No one is attacking your new friends from the hood."

103

I move my index finger up and down in front of Cheyenne's face, like I'm pressing a button.

"What are you doing?" Cheyenne asks.

"This is me pressing the dislike button on you! I never knew you were a mean girl. When did you get to be a mean girl?"

"I'm not mean, but there is a certain level of decorum I expect out of my friends. And I can just see Kellita's ghetto self causing drama at the party."

"They're actually not ghetto at all. She and Kellin work really hard and she's going to college for Computer Science."

"Someone said she has like three kids. How is she going to college?"

"She has two babies. They're twins. She ended up with a two for one special. That doesn't make her any less smart than we are. I'm going to need you to be a bigger person than that."

"Listen. If I didn't think your new friends were okay, I would've tried to talk you out of inviting them. It's cool."

"Cool. But what about you and Todrick? Are you going together? As a couple?"

Cheyenne bursts into laughter. "No. I do not like Todrick."

I grin, but keep my comments to myself. I know that Cheyenne likes Todrick, but for some reason she's placed herself in denial, and that is not a good place to be!

"What's wrong with Todrick? He's cute. His hair is so dark and curly. He's got the best hair of all the boys in the school."

Cheyenne holds up a little pink dress and says, "This is what you should wear. I have some bracelets that would really set this off. And I like this one shoulder strap thing."

"But it's cold. I'll need a jacket with that."

"So wear a jacket. Just take it off when we get inside the party."

"Okay. So what about Todrick? Don't you think he's cute? He's awesome, right?"

Cheyenne places the dress on the table and gives me an evil look. "Did Todrick put you up to this? I know he likes me. He's been on me for a minute."

"So, why don't you give him some play? He's a great guy! How you gonna leave him hanging like that?"

"I'm not. As soon as he does it the right way, then I might just holla back."

I shake my head. "Cheyenne, what is he doing wrong? He doesn't read *Cosmo Girl*, you know."

"Whatever. This has nothing to do with *Cosmo Girl*, and everything to do with the fact that he's never once approached me for real, like a true gentleman."

"OMG! A true gentleman? Seriously?"

"Yes. That's what my daddy always says. The guy should approach me like a gentleman."

"What does that mean? And even more impor-tantly, does Todrick know what it means?"

"I don't know exactly. But I have a feeling I'll know it when I see it."

I shrug and pick up the pink dress. "Okay, I'll rock this dress on one condition."

"Ha! I don't do conditions. I don't care what you wear!"

"Cheyenne . . . come on!"

"All right. What are your stupid conditions?"

"Just promise me that if Todrick makes his move, that you don't embarrass him."

Cheyenne smiles. "If Todrick makes a move . . . like a true gentleman would . . . I will not embar-rass him."

OMG! Dealing with two friends with crushes is the worst thing ever. But, it really is helping me get over Mario.

Something else that's helping me get over Mario is my brand new friend. I know that Kellin has drama going on right now, and I'm not ready for a new boyfriend anyway. But, the fact that I'm very excited to see him and hang out with him is a good sign.

It's a sign that maybe, just maybe, I'll stop bursting into tears when I think about my first date with Mario. And that everything, somewhere down the line, is going to be okay.

# 12

Our class has parties for everything, and New Year's Eve is no different. Everyone's at the Main Event with party clothes on like we're on Times Square watching the ball drop. There are a handful of parent chaperones to make sure that no one does anything crazy. I'm glad they're here, because my parents wouldn't let me come if they weren't.

Cheyenne and I walk in together, both looking too cute to be coming to a place that serves greasy pizza and soft drinks. We should be going out on the town or something.

"Good! We got here early enough to grab a table. I hate when we have to stand up. My feet already hurt in these shoes." Cheyenne directs my attention to her very cute Jessica Simpson black sequined stilettos.

As we sit down, I scan the room, looking for trouble—namely Mario and Dorie. I wonder if

108 someone has told Mario about the game yet. I made my threat to Mandy and Ashley a few days ago. I'm sure it's gotten back to Dorie that I said I was going to spill her secret.

I see Dorie's crew, but not Dorie. And there's no sign of Mario either. Hmm . . . this is all bad.

Todrick walks into the party and waves at us. Cheyenne looks away like she's uninterested, but I do see the faint smile on her face, so I know that she is.

"Your boy's here," I say.

"Shut up! He's not my boy yet."

Kellin and Kellita walk in right behind Todrick and I stand up to wave them over. Todrick takes his time getting over to the table. He's stopping at different groups and saying hello. It's cracking me up, because some of the people he's talking to aren't even cool with him! He's just stalling!

I give Kellita a hug when they get to the table and Kellin gives me a one armed hug, kinda like a 'hey buddy' hug. It's cool. I don't think I can handle anything outside of buddy right now.

"So, Kellita and Kellin, this is my best friend Cheyenne. Cheyenne, meet Kellin and Kellita."

Cheyenne gives them a wide and genuine smile. I feel relieved, because after that conversation we had earlier, I didn't know how she was going to come at them.

"Nice to meet y'all," Cheyenne says. "I've heard

so much about both of you. Zoey can't stop talking about how great y'all are."

Kellita bursts into laughter. "Well, she must be talking about me, because she and Kellin get into an argument just about every other day at the restaurant. She called him ignorant right out the box!"

"Those are not arguments," Kellin explains. "They are debates. We debate stuff. Zoey is pretty good, but I'm better. Sometimes I let her feel like she's getting the upper hand, but then I swoop in at the end and remind her that she doesn't."

"Boy please," I say. "I always have the upper hand."

Kellin beams at me and then looks around. "Where's your other friend, Todrick?"

"He's here, but he's making his rounds. He'll be over here in a minute," I reply. I'm not going to put him on blast to these newcomers. They don't need to know that he's nervous about Cheyenne.

"That's not who I want to see," Kellita says. "Where's the fool that played you for the cheerleader?"

Cheyenne snickers under her breath. "The *fool* is nowhere to be seen, and he probably won't show up."

"He'll be here," I reply. "The entire glee club is supposed to be here."

Todrick finally gets to the table and gives hugs and daps all the way around.

"I feel like I know y'all already," Todrick says to

Kellin and Kellita. "I heard y'all been teaching my homegirl how to cook."

"I already knew how to cook Todrick. Don't play."

"Hot dogs and Jiffy corn muffins is not cooking, baby," Kellita says.

She looks down and checks her phone. I see her face go from jolly to alarmed in an instant.

"Is everything okay, Kellita?" I ask.

She sighs. "My daughter has a fever. I think she might have an ear infection or something."

Cheyenne lifts an eyebrow and looks at me. I know her well enough to know what she's thinking. Kellita has drama that we don't even wish we knew about.

"I gotta go make a phone call. I'll be right back."

Kellin looks after his sister with concern, then with a smile on his face, turns to Todrick and asks, "How did you end up with two hot girls for best friends? I need you to teach me a thing or two."

"It's not all it's cracked up to be," Todrick says. "You have to hear all about their boyfriends, and their ex-boyfriends. And then don't think you can transition that into a date. They're looking at you crazy."

Cheyenne looks away, and tries to pretend that she's not in the conversation.

"Who's looking at you crazy?" I ask. "You've never asked me out on a date. I would've gone."

"Yeah, right, Ms. Mario, oh Mario, where for art

thou Mario?" Todrick says. "A brotha like me would've been on the sidelines looking in."

Kellin says, "Mario is over and done with now, right? So go ahead and get your mack on!"

"Well, honestly, I'm not really feeling Zoey," Todrick says.

"Forget you, too then!" I reply.

"And plus," Todrick continues, "I'm not much of a mack. I'm more of a gentleman, you know?"

As much as I try to contain my smile, I can't. Cheyenne kicks me under the table, and I pretend to not feel it.

"I do think it's possible to transition from friend to boyfriend," Kellin says. "It just takes some time and probably the opportunity. Like maybe your friend has to deal with a really thoughtless jerk to appreciate you."

"Or maybe she'll just open her eyes one day," Cheyenne says, "and see you like she's never seen you before."

My eyes widen as a huge grin blossoms onto Todrick's face. If that wasn't an opening, then I don't know what was.

"Kellin," I say. "Can I ask you a question in private? It's about work."

Kellin gives me a weird look and then says, "Okay . . ."

I pull Kellin away from the table and walk him over to the buffet that's full of goodies. I hand him a plate.

"I'm not hungry," he says. "I ate before I came."

"Just get a plate anyway. We need to stay away

from the table long enough for Todrick to make his move."

"His move? Oh. Oh! He likes Cheyenne?"

I nod. "Yep. They've been arguing back and forth forever. I think they're just now realizing that there is a crush factor going on."

"How's that gonna work if they hook up? Will your little trio be ruined?"

I shrug. "Probably. They'll more than likely gross me out on a consistent basis. Especially, since I don't have a boyfriend right now. At least I do have other friends."

"Don't look now, but there's a latino looking dude staring at you."

I chuckle. "Really? Put your arm around me."

"Somebody is being messy," Kellin says.

"Can I please, just have this moment?"

Kellin smiles and does me one better than putting his arm around me. He hugs me from behind and kisses my cheek. Okay, I know this is pretend . . . but dang . . . I could get to like this.

"Mission accomplished," Kellin says. "Your friend just stormed away. Was it Mario?"

"Yep." I entangle myself from Kellin's embrace and start loading appetizers onto my plate. When I'm nervous, I eat. Mario staring at me with Kellin and then getting mad about it makes me totally nervous.

"Are you okay?" Kellin asks.

"Yes. I just didn't expect him to be mad about me with someone else. What does that mean? Does it mean he still likes me?"

Kellin shrugs. "Not necessarily. Guys are territorial, you know? He might not want to get back with you, but he's probably still mad to think you're with someone else. Especially someone as fly as me."

I laugh out loud. "You sure are feeling yourself."

"You know. That's what us QB-1s do. Ooh, look at that girl checking me out."

I look up and see that Dorie is scoping Kellin out. This is hilarious! She's looking at Kellin like she wants to throw down some serious female mackification (I know this is a made up word. Just roll with me.) even though she's posted up with her boyfriend, Ethan. Surprisingly, I'm only a little bit jealous. That probably means that Kellin is safely tucked away in friend space, which is exactly where I need him to be.

"She just wants you because she thinks you're with me. She likes picking over my leftovers."

"Oh, wow! That's the girl who took your man?"

"Yeah, one of those irresistible cheerleaders."

Kellin checks her out once more and then says. "Well, if you ask me, your boy took a downgrade. She's not all that."

Now I could give Kellin a hug for real! I sooo needed to hear that from an incredibly hot boy. Even if he is just a friend.

"Maybe he's realizing that! Maybe that's why he's all up in my mix."

"True," Kellin says. "Oh, wait . . . cheerleader girl is coming over here."

OMG! I don't want to have any confrontations with her. Not tonight. I'm not in the mood to be embarrassed.

Dorie walks right up to us with Ethan following at her heels like a little puppy dog. She looks Kellin up and down. "I know you. QB-1 at Skyline High School."

"Yeah, that would be me. Kellin Owens."

She snatches his plate away. "This is a Lewisville High party, paid for by our student council. No one said you could bring guests Zoey."

Oh, no this heifer didn't. I feel my body temperature go from cool as a cucumber to hot enough to scald a heifer in two seconds flat.

"It's okay," Kellin says. "I wasn't really hungry anyway."

I snatch another plate and give it to Kellin. "I've raised more money than you for student council. I've washed cars, delivered orders at Sonic, and sold candy. Back up out of my friend's face."

"Or what? Are you going to throw a bowling ball at me? Or run me over with a go-kart? That's what you were trying to do, right? Run Mario over with a go-kart. You are psychotic, so maybe I should be afraid."

Her voice is so loud that she's drawing a crowd. My hands start to tremble. This is GoKart

Heaven all over again. Why is she putting me on blast? I haven't done that to her.

Kellin takes the plate from my hand and sits it down on the buffet. "Come on, Zoey. You don't have to take this. I know a spot where we can get much better food than these dried up chicken wings. Let's roll out."

I glance over at Cheyenne and Todrick. They're totally boo-ed up, so they don't need me at all.

"Okay, Kellin. I'm game."

He whispers in my ear as we walk away from them. "Hold your head up. Don't cry. She's not worth it."

We pass Kellita on her way back in, and she gives us a sad look. "My baby's fever spiked," she says. "I need to go home."

Kellin says, "It's cool, we were going back that way anyhow. Drama."

"Drama? With who? Your ex-boyfriend?"

I shake my head. "No. His new girlfriend."

"Where's she?"

"Don't worry about it, Lita. Come on."

Kellita looks like she wants to go back into the party and regulate. I think it would be all bad, so I take her arm.

"Kellita, it's cool, really. I just want to leave."

As we're walking out the door, Mario runs up behind us. "Why didn't you tell me, Zoey? Why didn't you tell me about Dorie's game?"

"I know you're not seriously asking me that question, Mario. You played me, and then you played yourself. I don't have anything to do with that."

Kellin puts one hand on Mario's chest and pushes him back. "I'm gonna need you to back up a little bit, dude."

Mario looks down at Kellin's hand and then says, "This your bodyguard or something?"

"No, he's my friend. Did you break up with her? Did she lose?"

Mario shakes his head. "No, she didn't. She won. Apparently, Ethan's *geek* found out about the game first, and broke up with him."

"That's so unfortunate . . . but we're about to get up out of here. I'll see you at school."

I walk away from Mario and the Main Event feeling pretty satisfied with myself for not laughing in Mario's face or trying to make him feel as bad as he made me feel.

In the parking lot, Kellin says, "You did great back there, Zoey. You've got it going on."

"I do? Thanks."

"Yeah. If I didn't have my own drama going on, I might just be trying to get your number. You're pretty, smart, and classy. The whole package."

I don't respond with words as I get into the backseat of Kellin's car. I respond with a smile. Who knows if Kellin and I will ever get together? Maybe, maybe not. But I like that the possibility is there.

What I like even better is that I can think of

Mario now, and not cry. And if he tries to get back, I've got absolutely no holler for him at all. Sweet!

I've survived! My first boyfriend and my first break up, and I'm still in one piece. A pretty, smart, and classy piece too.

On to the next one!

"Let's roll out," I say from the backseat. "I've got a taste for some chicken!"

# SWAG

## KEVIN ELLIOTT

# 1
———

When I first saw him, he was in front of the C building. He stood in the middle of a crowd of boys, looking real fly. Wavy hair, chocolate skin, nice teeth, with the body of a basketball player. All the other boys laughed at his jokes. The center of attention. He was so sexy! I knew all the other girls at the school must have been thinking the same thing. I didn't have a chance with him. Besides, he looked like the kind of guy that would break my heart. The kind of guy that my mom wouldn't approve of. She had told me more than once to quit chasing pretty boys and she hated jocks. She believed all jocks were bad and she wanted to spare me a heartbreak, but mom would have to learn that I have to grow up. While I don't like getting hurt, I know that's part of growing up.

I would find out from my friend Malaka Brown,

who walked up to me and said, "DeMarco Mobley likes you."

I said, "Who?" That name sounded familiar, but I didn't know who that was until she pointed to the same boy that I had been looking at earlier. How crazy is that?

"Him, over there." She pointed to my dream man who stood in front of the main building this morning, with the crowd of boys. Still the center of attention. Malaka had to be lying. There was no way that boy wanted me, he could have anybody he wanted. He had to have a girlfriend; there was no way he *didn't* have a girlfriend. I couldn't believe that.

Candace, my best friend since kindergarten, said, "I heard he lives in the valley with his brothers. Heard his mother died."

I just wondered how everybody knew who this guy was and I didn't. How did I overlook Mr. Milk Chocolate?

Malaka was popping gum and blowing huge bubbles. It was so annoying that ordinarily I would say something about it, but I wanted to hear more about how DeMarco wanted me.

"Yeah, I was walking past his boys and 'em and he was talking about how sexy you are," Malaka said.

I smiled. "They were talking about me?"

"Yes, Zori, but it wasn't them, it was him. DeMarco, he was the one that said you were fine."

"Really?" I said. I didn't want to seem too excited. Funny how God works. I was just thinking about what it would be like to be his girlfriend. Walking hand and hand with Mr. Fine, making all the little chicken heads mad because he picked me. Mad because I was wearing his letterman jacket, assuming he had one. He sure looked like an athlete. Mad because I had the tallest, best looking boy in the whole school. Well, at least in my eyes.

"Zori, you know you want to smile."

I tried hard not to, but a wide smile covered my face. How real is that? If I didn't smile, my girls knew I would be faking.

Malaka said, "So, are you gonna talk to him?

"Mom said never to chase a boy. Let them do the chasing and besides, if he wants me, he knows where I'm at."

"Your mama obviously hasn't seen DeMarco Mobley," Malaka said.

I looked over at DeMarco and the boys again. Our eyes met briefly before I turned away. I didn't want him to catch me staring, but at the same time, I wanted him to know I was interested. I cast a quick glance at him again, hoping my eyes gave him the okay to make his move.

"I heard he sells packs," Malaka said.

"Packs of what?"

Malaka laughed. "You know packs, like in drugs. He's a drug dealer, I swear you girls are so square." I hated when Malaka said that. Her tone made it seem as though me and Candace were naive. Malaka was from the hood, but she didn't act ghetto. She actually made really good grades and she'd vowed that she would be the first person in her family to go to college. But I had to admit she was a little bit more street smart than me. I was more street smart than Candace, but that wasn't saying much. Paris Hilton was more street smart than Candace. Though she was my best friend, Candace could be very uppity at times. She only dated boys who came from a two-parent home. Said she wanted somebody with the same values that she had and she wasn't going to compromise.

"Really?" Candace said. "That's a shame. Looks like he just blew his chance with my girl, because there is no way we're going to get caught up in that kind of foolishness." She glanced at me. Candace waited on me to agree with her. I didn't. I didn't know if that was true. As far as I was concerned, it was a rumor.

"Yeah. I mean, look at how fly he always is. He always has the latest shoes, the flyest gear. Those True Religions he's wearing cost like three hundred dollars. Two hundred dollar sneakers. His watch looks like it cost about a thousand dollars. What seventeen-year-old can afford clothes like that?"

"Maybe his parents have money."

"His mom died and his two older brothers are drug dealers."

124

My mom would kill me if I dated a hustler. I hoped that he wasn't, but then there was a part of me that hoped that he did hustle. It was something about the life that thrilled me.

Malaka popped her gum loudly, grabbing my attention. I wished she hadn't spoken about DeMarco in front of Candace. I knew Candace wouldn't tell my mom, but if I hooked up with DeMarco, I knew she would try her best to break us up. She would hate on me especially if I got any gifts from him. Thinking of my future gifts from DeMarco made me think of Michelle Agurs, a girl from my track team who often received money and gifts from her hustling boyfriend. Girls in my neighborhood didn't do that—they were goody two-shoes. Our parents had told us to go out with nice boys. The kind who opened doors for us. The kind who said yes sir and no sir. Not disrespectful guys and not wannabe gangsters.

Once, when me and Mom were at Home Depot, we ran across one of my classmates, Jeremy Jones. I was hoping that he wouldn't see us, but I'm never that lucky. Not only did he see me, he came right up to me.

"That's yo mama?"

"Yeah, Jeremy."

"Yo mama fine as hell."

I almost choked when he said that, but it didn't

surprise me because of the way he acted in school. But Mom was in total shock, looking at me in total disbelief. In her day, boys didn't act like that. They would never curse in front of someone's parents and most of my friends wouldn't either, but Jeremy was from the projects. Not all project kids acted like that, but Jeremy had been a juvenile delinquent since he was fourteen. He had got sent away to a boy's home for thirty days for assaulting some white kids, and ever since, he'd been in and out of trouble. He liked me for a while, even came to my house a time or two, but I had never let him meet my mom for fear of how he would act. He confirmed my fear when he saw me in Home Depot that day, acting exactly how I knew he would act. Mom said later she wanted to slap the taste out of Jeremy's mouth.

I looked down at my phone: It was Jay, and it was the third time he'd called this morning. I sent him to voice mail. My mom glanced at my phone, being nosey. "Who keeps calling you back to back like that?"

"Jay."

Mom smiled. She liked Jay, thought he was a nice boy. Wanted me to date him. I liked him too, but Jay just didn't have the edge I wanted in a boyfriend. He couldn't dress. Just didn't have swagger. Even so, I'd gone out with him twice. He was real courteous and respectful. I knew he was a decent person and an ambitious guy, but he just didn't excite me. Didn't do it for me.

"So what does he want?"

"I don't know. I didn't answer, remember?"

She frowned. "Why didn't you answer him? He must wanna tell you something important. I think you should at least answer the phone."

"I'll call him back later."

She shook her head. "I'm telling you Jay's a keeper."

I hated when she talked like that. I'm only sixteen. I'm not thinking about settling down, and if I were, it sure wouldn't be with Jay.

"Mom, can you just cut it out?"

"I'm just saying he's a nice boy with a good future ahead of him."

"How do you know he has a good future? Nobody knows the future."

"Zori, you getting smart with me?"

"I'm just saying can I pick the person I want to date?"

"What happened to that other boy you dated? The one that drove the blue Honda Accord?"

"Malik?"

"Yeah, I liked him, too." I sighed. "Dude only had like two pair of shoes."

Mom busted out a loud laugh. "You are *so* superficial."

I turned my head and rolled my eyes. I knew from experience that if she saw me rolling my eyes at her, there'd be serious trouble. She was always saying I was superficial, but she made me that way. I got my first Louis bag when I was fourteen and my Daddy had always said never date a guy who had less than me. They were the culprits, not me.

# 2

I was walking down the hall at school when somebody grabbed my booty. I spun around, prepared to smack back. Nobody touches this booty. But when I turned, I saw his tall chocolate fine self. His braids were like black snakes on his head, falling perfectly on his shoulder. When he smiled, I almost forgot that he'd practically violated me with that booty grab. I managed to say, "What's your problem?"

His smile widened. "You know you liked that."

"Is that how you approach girls?"

"The ones I like."

It took all my power to hold back my smile. He said he liked me!

He pulled his iPhone from his book bag. "What's your phone number?"

"Don't you want to know my name?"

"Come on, shorty. Cut it out. I know your name and you know mine."

I laughed. "What makes you so sure?"

"I'm popular, and you're one of the finest chicks at this school."

I liked this dude's swag. So confident, almost cocky, and a little arrogant. I almost felt like doing whatever he said. Almost. "Hey, before we go any further, apologize for grabbing my butt."

He laughed and looked me in the eyes. "Are you serious?"

"Of course I am."

"OK, shorty. I'm sorry."

"Cut the 'shorty' stuff out."

"Now you tripping—that's just the way I talk."

I had him hooked, so I gave him my number. "Call me before ten on school days."

"What, you gotta curfew?" He laughed.

"No, I have a lot more on my mind than talking on the phone. I have to get my rest. I'm not trying to come to school all tired."

The moment I stepped in the door, Jay called again. "Jay, what's up?"

"Been trying to reach you."

"Yeah, I've been kind of busy. Lots of home-work, you know."

"Well, you know you can ask me if you ever need any help with anything."

I knew what he said was true. Jay was smart and he was taking advanced classes as well. Even

Kevin Elliott

though he was a very nice guy, I didn't want to be alone with Jay. I didn't want him to get the wrong idea.

"Thanks for the offer, Jay. I will keep that in mind."

"No problem."

Okay, so now I'm wondering why he called and if I can get him off the phone quickly. "What's up?"

There was an awkward silence over the phone and that's one thing that I hated about our conversations. They were full of awkward silences. It made me bored with him. It was like he didn't know what to say, or if he did know what to say, he sure wasn't saying it. Almost like I made him nervous and I didn't like nervousness—confidence turned me on. DeMarco Mobley turned me on. Finally, I said again, "Jay, what's up?"

"Well, I just wondering if you would go to the Christmas dance with me."

"The Christmas dance?" I squeaked out. I knew what he was talking about, but I had to buy time. Had to think of a reason that I couldn't go. I could tell him somebody had asked me already, but that would hurt his feelings . . . and he would see that I was lying because I wouldn't be there. Maybe I should tell him that I didn't have a thing to wear.

"Yeah, I talked to my Dad, asked him if he would rent a limo. He said he would."

Dang it, if his daddy went through the trouble of getting a limo, I knew that he could easily persuade him to buy me a dress. My lie about not having a thing to wear would not work and Jay knew my mom. He knew she could easily buy me a dress. I couldn't think of an excuse to give him. No legitimate excuse.

"A limo to the Christmas dance. Nobody rents a limo to the Christmas dance, Jay. This ain't the Prom."

"Not everybody can take a dime like you to the dance. You deserve the best."

I was blushing. Fascinated that he found me fascinating. I just wish he had a little bit more edge.

"Hey, you didn't tell your dad that I was going with you to the dance, did you?"

"No . . . why?"

"Just asking," I mumbled. The real reason was I sure didn't need the added pressure of him telling his dad that I would go. I was really struggling now. Why couldn't I come up with an excuse?

"So, can I count you in?"

"Hmm . . . Jay, give me to the end of the week to get back with you."

Awkward silence again.

"Jay, are you there?"

"I was just thinking there must be somebody else you had in mind for the dance. It's okay if you don't wanna go with me, just say it."

"Just give me to the end of the week."

\* \* \*

Not ten minutes later, DeMarco called and said he wanted to meet. I suggested that we meet at Tony's, this little pizza parlor around the corner from my house.

I heard him when he pulled up in a Cadillac Escalade with rims, blasting a Lil Wayne song. All the patrons in the restaurant heard him as well. The music was so loud, I was embarrassed.

He wore new Timbs, True Religions, and a Polo sweater. I was almost blinded by the diamonds he had in each ear and the blinged out watch on his wrist. Not the same watch that he was wearing the day I met him.

When DeMarco walked in, I was standing at the counter. I ordered a slice of cheese pizza. He ordered the same. I had a Diet Coke and he had a Coke. To pay for our order, he dug in his pocket and pulled out a wad of bills, hundreds and twenties. He peeled off a twenty and handed it to the clerk.

An elderly white couple behind us looked at us and the bills in DeMarco's hands, but didn't say anything. They didn't have to say anything. I knew just by the looks they wore on their faces that they wondered where he got all that money and I was a little embarrassed by the situation. DeMarco didn't pay anybody any mind. I knew he was the type of guy that didn't care what people said or thought about him and that was a good thing, but

I'd wished he didn't pull a whole bank roll of cash to pay for eleven dollars worth of food.

"Why are you drinking diet soda?" he sounded disgusted.

I love my diet soda. I never had regular soda—my Mom had been giving me diet soda since I was a baby. She said she didn't want a fat daughter. A girl's gotta watch her figure, you know.

I guess he decided to back down, 'cause he said, "I'll do that." Whatever that means. He smiled, then winked.

When the pizza came, we sat in a booth in the back of the restaurant.

"Damn, you looking good, shorty." His voice was so seductive. Made me think I was as delicious as the pizza.

I had to admit I did look good. I had put on my skin tight Seven jeans and a designer sweater. My heels were from Aldo, but they were banging brown lizard skinned in purple. Five inches. I could barely walk, but they made me look so much taller than my five foot six inches. They made mc look really grown too. I'd worn a pair of flats when I left the house 'cause my Mom would flip if she knew about these killer heels.

"Thank you," I said nonchalantly. Didn't want him to think I was feeling myself. "So, how can you afford a car like that?" I asked, nodding my head toward his Escalade outside the restaurant.

Instead of answering, he stirred his Coke with

Kevin Elliott

his straw. Suddenly, he was acting kind of shy and it was endearing coming from a guy with so much confidence. I was seeing a side of him that I'd never seen before. Hmmm . . .

I tried my question again. "How come you're driving such an expensive truck?"

His smile covered his whole face. I saw dimples. "Since when is driving a nice car against the law?"

"It's not, I was just asking. We're about the same age. That's a lot of car for someone our age to handle."

"Of course we are." He'd only addressed half of what I said.

Looks like I was going to have to run this conversation. "You don't have a job, and if you did have a job, you couldn't possibly afford a car like that unless your parents are rich." Please, please, let his parents be loaded. I want to hit the jackpot!

"I ain't got no parents. Mom is dead and I've never seen that deadbeat of a father of mine."

I didn't know what to say to that. Though my dad didn't live with me, he was my heart and I loved him very much. We just had a situation where he and my mom weren't meant to be together, but I was still glad that he was in my life. I couldn't imagine a life without either one of them. I wouldn't touch the subject of his parents unless he wanted to talk about them.

I moved the conversation back to the start. "So, how did you get the money to get a car like that?"

"It's a truck, shorty," he said sarcastically. Okay, his swag was starting to dull.

"Car, truck, whatever. You know what I mean." I bit into my pizza. I was hungry. It was a big bite. I was not the type of girl that tried to be cute around boys. I like to eat and I didn't care who saw me.

"It's my brother's truck."

Finally. "Really?"

"Yeah, he's twenty-two."

"So what does he do?"

"I don't know what he does. What's up with all these questions?"

I ignored that last bit and continued. "You don't know what your brother does?" At that point, I knew the rumors must have been true about his brother being a drug dealer. How else could a twenty-two year old afford a truck like that? How did he not know what his brother did for a living?

He sipped his drink. Face went blank. I could tell he was thinking about something. Perhaps he was thinking of a lie to tell me. I'd thought about what Malaka said about him moving packs. I knew he would never tell me that. I would never find out the truth about him and his brother, at least not today. His brother was still young, still had his whole life ahead of him, too. It was really a shame.

"Shorty, that's not important. Let's just enjoy the moment."

"Cool."

"So, what do you like to do?"

"I like to hoop, but I didn't play this year."

"Why not?"

"The practice took up too much time and I have other stuff to do. I'm better than everybody on the team. I don't need no practice."

Hmm, he's too good for practice? Even Shaq practiced. He's fine, but he needs some reality. "Everybody needs practice."

"I'm the best," he insisted, so I let it go. Maybe he was, but since I hadn't seen him play, I didn't want to contradict him. I am sure he could play; he probably had a lot of raw talent. I wasn't about to get into it with him about why I think he needed practice; there was no way he was going to listen to me. I'm a girl, not a coach.

"So what happened? Did you get cut?"

He frowned and looked at me like I'd said something about his mother. I sipped my drink.

"I've never been cut from a team sport in my life."

"But you're not on the team."

"He kicked me off the team. Said I had an attitude."

"He cut you," I said, emphasizing cut. I don't know why I was baiting him.

He frowned at me. "Cut is when you're not

good enough. Now how can he cut the best player on the team?" He folded his pizza and took a bite. "Hell, they ain't paying anyway. So screw the coach and screw the team. I got more money than anybody on that team, including the coach.

Now really. Did he think he had enough money to have this kind of attitude? I'd seen guys like him before flashing a few bills here and there. He thought he was rich because he had nice clothes on and was driving his brother's truck. He talked big, but how long was his money? And more importantly, where did it come from? It was time for me to get some answers, and I wasn't going to play coy with it. "Where do you work?"

"I don't work. My brother gives me money."

"The brother that you don't know what he does, but he drives an Escalade."

He looked at me sharply. "Shorty got a smart mouth."

I smiled, not wanting to piss him off because I really did like him. He had potential. I just wanted to make sure I had all the facts. "I'm just trying to get to know you, that's all." I smiled sweetly.

"You asking all the wrong questions, though."

I bit into my pizza, not knowing what to say and trying to take my time finding the right response. I swallowed my food and flashed him my dimples. Guys were always distracted by my dimples.

He leaned forward, elbows on the table. "Listen, I don't want to talk about that wack team and

I don't want to talk about my brother. Let's talk about you and me." He leaned back in his seat and gave me a sexy smile. "You and me look good together. I can see me taking you places."

Now that's what I'm talking about. Glad that we were moving on from sports—I'd have to find another in for finding out about his money situation—I said, "I know." Going places got me thinking about the upcoming dance. If I showed up as his date, the haters would lose their minds! Now, how can I get him to ask me out? "And I can definitely see you and me making the rounds. Since you're popular," I paused and flashed my dimples again, "and I'm the flyest chick you know," I paused at his laughter.

"Shorty, I see where this is going, so I'll stop you there. I'm not in to going to the dance. I wouldn't be caught dead at a corny school dance."

Whoa, then what's the point? "Why not?"

"Not my thing," he said and placed his elbows on the table again. Absolutely no table manners, and yet I was still intrigued. Somebody needs to come up with a cure for my bad boy attraction, 'cause I was trying to hang on to his arrogant, sexy self. I wasn't going to give up yet.

"But I was thinking about going." I leaned forward, my hands at my sides, letting the girls do the talking with me. "I know it may seem corny to you, but—"

"No. Dances is precisely what girls should do,

not gangstas. Imagine me at a dance in a tux looking like a clown." He laughed.

"So if girls are the only ones going to the
dance, how is it going to be fun and who is going
to escort the girls?"

"Those clown-type dudes."

I laughed. This guy had life all figured out. At
least in his world.

"So what makes you a gangster?"

He laughed again and bit into his pizza. Then
laughed some more.

"What are you laughing at?"

"You sound so white. 'So what makes you a
gangster?'" he mocked me in his best white
woman's voice.

"I sound white because I speak with proper
English?"

"Yep."

Now that made me mad. Folks had been telling
me that since elementary school, and I didn't find
it funny. And it was always the kids from the hood
that made fun of me. Said I sounded white because I pronounced words correctly.

"So are you going to answer my question?"

"I'm gangster because I'm not like you. I wasn't
born with a silver spoon in my mouth."

"Silver spoon, whatever." I laughed. "If that's
what you wanna believe." I shrugged. "If you're
not cool with the dance, fine. I already have a
date."

"So who you going to the dance with?"

"Jay Richmond asked me."

"Goofy ass Jay Richmond with the egg-shaped head? That's exactly what I meant . . . a clown-type dude."

"You know him?" I was so surprised. I never thought Jay and DeMarco would run in the same circles. How did they know each other? I wondered how they ever crossed paths. I knew Jay was on the basketball team; that had to be the connection, but Mr. DeMarco didn't want me to bring that subject up again and I didn't feel like arguing about something so meaningless.

"Yeah, I've been knowing the dude since we were eight, we played Pop Warner football together, Jay is on the basketball team and we're in the same advanced calculus class together."

Now I was confused. I thought he was a gangsta and how he's talking about a math class. "You are in advanced calculus?" My dismay was clear.

He smiled showing all his teeth and those dimples were showing again. "Just because I don't speak proper English like you doesn't mean that I'm not smart."

"Obviously you are smart, if you're in advanced calculus.

"Advanced English, too, sweetie." He grinned again.

I was impressed, I didn't even have advanced

English. Guys like him made me so mad. Smart guys, but wanted to pretend that they were dumb. Like that was cool or something.

"But yeah Jay asked me to go, I don't know if I'm going or not."

"Jay is a a'ight dude. Scared as hell of me though always have been, but Jay is not too much of a clown, not like some of those other dudes I hear that were going to the dance. I like Jay but he's scared of me though.

"Why must you be so damn aggressive?"

"I ain't aggressive, just throwing that tidbit of information out there."

"I didn't need it."

"I know what you need. In fact, I got what you need."

I played with my hair. I knew exactly what he meant because he was staring at my breasts when he said it. I pulled some lip gloss from my purse and applied it to my lips. He was in for a surprise, 'cause I wasn't givin' up the goodies.

"You don't need to put that on." He licked his lips suggestively.

"Why not—?"

He leaned across the table and leaned in for a kiss. Before he could put his tongue down my throat, I turned my head to the side so that his lips met the corner of my lips. That was as far as I'd let him get today, but I wondered if he was going to use that small peck to taunt Jay. I hoped he wouldn't.

Kevin Elliott

"So you and Jay going to the dance?"

"I don't know."

"Why not? I told you Jay is a good dude."

I looked away. I really didn't want to say anything bad about Jay because he was such a nice guy and I didn't want DeMarco to ever be able to tell Jay I said something bad about him. I didn't think that would be right. "The dance should be cool, I just haven't decided yet."

"Well, don't go."

"Jay's dad rented a limo."

DeMarco's eye's grew wide. "A limo for a Christmas dance? That's crazy, but Jay's family got bread. I think his dad is a doctor or something."

Okay, so he doesn't really know Jay. "A dentist."

"You see, that's a clown type move right there, renting a limo for a Christmas dance. When will these dudes learn that chicks don't appreciate stuff like that?"

I drew back in my seat. What girl wouldn't like a limo, even just to go around the block. "I wouldn't say all of that."

He looked me directly in the eye and said, "If I asked you to go to that dance, we wouldn't be going in no limo and guess what, there would be no debate. You would go."

I didn't answer.

Later that night, when my best friend Candace called, the first thing she asked was, "How was the date?"

"Exactly what I expected, but I did learn something about him."

"Like what?"

"He's a really smart guy, a little rough, but smart."

"Really?"

"Advanced classes and all."

"Yeah, I knew he was taking some advanced classes and he was really good at basketball, but the coach kicked him off the team because of that attitude."

"Yeah, he told me all about it. That's when I saw the crazy part of him."

Candace squealed in anticipation. "What do you mean?"

"He went into this whole spiel about how he didn't need to practice, how he was better than everybody on the team and he said screw the team. Screw the coach and nobody had more money than he had. The usual cocky stuff."

"Ha, ha!" Candace laughed loudly. "He sounds a little crazy. What you going to do with that?"

"Despite the crazy, I think deep inside he's a good guy. I don't think DeMarco is as crazy as he wants us to believe he is. I mean, he's sixteen. How tough can he be?"

"Well, I heard that his mother got killed in a crack house when he was like seven and his brothers are raising him and they are both drug dealers. I found this out from this girl named Avril who lives on the next street over from him in the Valley."

My mind went back to the Escalade he pulled up in. Went back to the questions I'd asked about him being a gangster and I felt sorry for him. I didn't know what I'd do if I'd lost my mother. "Yeah, I think he has a few issues, but I don't think that makes him a bad guy."

"He's a drug dealer," Candace reminded me. "He's doing that all on his own."

"I know," I said softly. I didn't want it to be that way, but that's the way it was. Knowing about his family situation was making it easy for me to fall for him. I knew Candace disapproved, but I was the one dating him, and I liked him. I just didn't want Candace to run her mouth to my mother. Lord, the last thing I needed was for my mother to find out.

At school the next morning, Jay stood by my locker. He looked good today. He wore a purple and turquoise sweater and some cargo pants. The Louis Vuitton shoes were to die for. Dude actually looked appealing—he'd obviously swag. He was still a long way from DeMarco, but I was feeling his new look . . . until he opened his mouth.

"So why haven't you called me to let me know if you're going to go to the dance?"

He sounded so pathetic, almost desperate. No confidence at all. He needed to go buy him some self esteem to go with his gear.

"I said I would hit you up on *Friday*." I was really not feeling like I needed to explain this to him. He wasn't my boyfriend.

146

No response. He just stood there with this stupid look on his face. When he finally moved aside, I opened my locker.

"*Today* is Friday," he said.

"I know, and I was gonna call you later." I put my books in my locker, grabbed my gym shoes, then closed the door.

He leaned against the locker and blocked me in. "Listen, Zori. You gotta go to this dance with me. I know you were unsure before but you gotta go with *me*."

"Why?"

"I told my parents you were going with me."

"What . . . why did you do that, Jay? That's got to be the dumbest thing you've ever done." Now I felt almost obligated to go to the dance with him. But that had to be his plan. He would tell his parents so I would feel obligated to go to the dance with him. And I knew he would also tell my mom. And here it comes . . .

"I don't know, it just kind of slipped out. My parents were asking if I had a date. I said yeah and then when they asked if I had a picture of you, I showed them your Facebook page."

"O. M. G. You did not just put me out there like that."

He dropped his head. He really looked sad. He liked me but I didn't really like him. That to me

Kevin Elliott

was one of the worst feelings, when you liked somebody and they didn't like you. I had been in Jay's shoes before. But I was still pissed that he had told his parents that I was going to the dance with him.

I pushed his arm away from the locker. I didn't like the fact that he had blocked me in. Mr. Jay Carter had blocked me in twice. At my locker and the Christmas dance. While I could walk around him at my locker, there was no escaping the Christmas dance and he knew this. I didn't like that he was trying to force me to go with him. I felt bad for the guy, but I didn't like this guilt trip.

I took a deep breath, then said, "Hey, I'll go. I will go with *you*." I had to wrap my mind around this new plan. Though I was going to the dance with the wrong date, it was up to me on whether I'd enjoy myself.

"Really?" A huge grin covered his face. The way the dude was smiling, you would think he'd just gotten the new iPhone or something.

"Yeah, Jay, but we're going to the dance and straight home." I didn't want him to think this was a romantic date. Far from it.

"That's fine with me." He was still smiling hard. It was hard to not smile back, so I finally smiled back.

"Gotta get to gym class. I will talk to you later."

# 3

I didn't hear from or see DeMarco for the rest of the week. I wondered what was going on with him, but I wasn't about to play myself running behind him and getting up in his business, so I fell back and did me for the rest of the week. Finally, on Friday night, DeMarco called and said he wanted to go out.

"Shorty, let's make this a double date. You got a friend you can bring along?"

I hated double dates, but I needed a reason to wear my new dress from BCBG that I had gotten from Dad for my birthday. It was a beautiful electric blue with a black belt. I wanted to wear it with my mom's black Jimmy Choo shoes. I even had an electric blue thong that DeMarco was not going to see.

I invited Candace and DeMarco's friend was Lil

Jimmy from DeMarco's neighborhood. Lil Jimmy was only five foot six inches, but he had a huge attitude and was funny as hell.

When DeMarco pulled up to my house, Candace and I were ready to go. I rode shotgun, while Candace and Lil Jimmy claimed their space in the backseat. Before we pulled away from the curb, Lil Jimmy was telling stories about him and DeMarco. They had known each other since they were babies. Their moms had pushed them in strollers together. They were two months apart, with Jimmy being a couple of months older. Out the corner of my eye, I could see Lil Jimmy occasionally put his hand on Candace's thigh.

Jimmy was telling us about the time DeMarco got in trouble in grade school. "So this dude peed in a milk carton beside his nap mat."

"What? Why?" I asked, giggling. This story was getting interesting.

DeMarco said, "My mom told me she was gonna whip my butt if I had pissed in my clothes again."

I laughed hard, imagining a little DeMarco peeing in a milk carton, then laying back down on his little mat.

"So you'd rather deal with the teacher than your mom?" Candace asked.

"Hell yeah. My mom didn't play."

"Yeah, I miss Ms. Brenda." Lil Jimmy said. "But dude, my mom is now your mom." I could tell he meant it. DeMarco and Lil Jimmy clearly were like brothers. "You know she calls you her son. She washes your clothes and feeds you whenever you want something to eat. She trusts you more than she trusts me and she's said that on more than one occasion."

DeMarco laughed. "Yeah, his mom and my mom had known each other since they were kids. They were close, too. Almost like sisters, and since I don't really deal with my aunties, his mom is like my mama."

But I wondered if he really looked at Jimmy's mom like a mother. I couldn't imagine that they could have the same bond. But I thought it was great that DeMarco had a mother figure in his life.

Jimmy said, "On a lighter note, I got some smoke," pulling out some weed the color of spinach. The smell was so strong that it burned my nose.

"I knew I smelled weed," Candace said.

Now, I didn't mind the smell of weed and didn't care if others smoked, but I knew Candace wouldn't be okay with it.

Jimmy smiled, showing all his teeth. "This is the bomb right here."

"Come on, dude, you're going to make all us go to jail because you wanna get high." Candace complained, giving Jimmy the stink eye.

"Go to jail?" Jimmy said, holding up his smoke sack. He shook his head. "This ain't enough to go to jail about, this is just some personal stuff. The most that will happen is that I will get a ticket. Nobody is going to jail and if we get pulled over, I will just stuff it in my crotch."

Candace snickered. "Stuffing it in your crotch would be a genius move if they couldn't smell. I've been smelling this stuff since I got in the car."

This double date had officially hit the rocks.

When Lil Jimmy rolled up a cigar-sized blunt, I turned to DeMarco. "He's not going to smoke that, is he?"

Candace leaned in toward me and said, "We don't smoke." She looked at me.

"Nope, we sure don't," I agreed.

"What?" Jimmy said. His expression said *You have got to be kidding, right?* "I thought everybody smoked. At least everybody in my circle smokes."

I looked at DeMarco. "You smoke?"

"From time to time, I blaze."

Jimmy chuckled. "I blaze every day."

DeMarco probably blazed every day too if Jimmy was his best friend.

"Put the weed up, Jimmy. They don't wanna smoke."

"Naw, I will smoke by myself," Jimmy said.

The look on Candace's face made me feel that I had to stop Jimmy from sparking.

"Hey Jimmy, I don't want that stuff all in my clothes," I said.

"Stop the car, man. I'll get out and smoke."

"Not now, Jimmy. Just relax, man. We can do that later," DeMarco said.

Just then I realized I had no idea where we were headed. We'd left my neighborhood behind a while ago and were near the mall. In the visor's mirror, it looked like Jimmy was stuffing the plastic baggie back in his pocket.

"So what's next?" he leaned toward Candace and wrapped his hand around her waist. She didn't stop him so I knew she was cool with him now that he'd put away his weed. Otherwise, she would have checked him right on the spot. I'd seen her slap dudes for feeling on her.

Just then I remembered that Candace's parents were out of town.

"Candace, let's go to your house and watch some Dave Chappelle." I leaned toward DeMarco and flashed my dimples. "And get acquainted more," I added just for him.

"I'd like that." Jimmy grinned, and I peeked his hand moving between Candace's legs.

Candace slapped his jaw.

"What was that for, shorty?"

Candace snapped, "Come on, Jimmy. I'm taller than you."

"Yeah, true . . . until we lay down. Then we're the same size."

I looked back at Candace. She was still smiling, but now I couldn't tell if she was enjoying herself. Jimmy had invaded her private space. She didn't know him like that. I was hoping that they could at least remain friendly; didn't want them to ruin me and DeMarco's time together.

DeMarco asked, "Can we at least get something to drink if we go back to her crib?"

Both Candace and I said, "No, we don't drink."

Jimmy sighed. "Yo, these girls are tripping, man."

DeMarco looked disgusted and I felt that the date was not going well. We had become bored with each other. I was used to this happening when I dated bad boys, especially when it came down to drinking and doing drugs. No matter how I might want to fit in, I just simply couldn't get with the whole drinking and drugging thing.

"So where do you live?" DeMarco asked Candace.

"Ridgewood Forest."

"What?" Jimmy screamed. His face was full of amazement. "You live over there, shorty?" He looked hard at Candace.

"Yeah, why?"

"No wonder this chick is acting all uppity."

"I ain't stuck up."

"I didn't say stuck up, I said uppity."

DeMarco said, "Damn, you're a rich chick, huh?"

"Hell, no. I wish I was rich." Candace said, then pulled me into it. "And Zori practically lives around the corner from me."

I knew she was going to say that. She always told people I lived around the corner from her because most of the people knew Ridgewood Forest had half-million-dollar homes and just so she wouldn't be singled out for being a snob she

would tell everybody I lived near her, too. Insinuating that I was rich. I did live close to her, but I
lived in another neighborhood with smaller homes,
but they were still nice compared to where
DeMarco and Jimmy were from.

"Rich bitches," Jimmy said.

"Bitches?" Candace said. She rolled her eyes at
Jimmy.

"Ha. Ha. Ha." Jimmy laughed faintly but nobody else did. De Marco's face showed he was annoyed.

"Nobody's rich. I'm from a single parent home,
my mom is a nurse struggling just like everybody
else," I said. This is the truth. Even though my
Dad was in my life and he supported me, we were
by no means rich. Candace's family was in a better
financial situation than we were, but she wasn't
rich either. But maybe it seemed like we were rich
compared to them.

"I'm rich!" DeMarco said emphatically as he
pulled out a wad of money like he'd pulled out at
the pizza parlor. The money was bound with rub-
ber bands and it just looked as if it was gained by
some sort of illegal activity.

I glanced at it. Looked to be at least a thousand
dollars in twenties. Not what I would call rich, but
it was still a lot of money for a high school kid.
The money was both a turn off and a turn on. A
turn off because he had bragged about what he
had and it turned me on because he had gotten
that money by any means necessary. But I wished

he would not have pulled that money out in front of Candace and I wished Jimmy had not pulled out his weed. I knew I would hear about this later from Candace. She'll try to chastise me and tell me why I shouldn't be with DeMarco. None of this I would want to hear. DeMarco and Jimmy had just given her ammunition for making her case.

"Can we just go to my house?" Candace said.

DeMarco finally agreed and followed Candace's directions to her house.

As we pulled up to her McMansion, I had to admit it did look like something from a rap video. Once inside, we all sat in the den and watched *Chappelle* until Jimmy said to Candace, "Show me around the mansion."

She giggled. "This ain't no mansion."

"It's the closest thing I'll ever get to a mansion. I'm telling you, shorty, I feel like I'm on *MTV Cribs*," Jimmy said as Candace stood and led him by the hand toward the basement.

When DeMarco and I were alone, he pulled out his phone. Was he about to call someone when I was sitting right up under him? Rude!

"Hey, babe. I wanna take a picture of us," he said. I guess I had the wrong idea. I moved in closer to him and wrapped my arm around his shoulders as he snapped a shot of us with his camera phone. I knew that picture was going to be hot 'cause we made a cute couple.

He stashed his phone in his pocket and put his hand on my thigh. I pushed it away and he did it again and I pushed it away again. He was *not* going to see my blue thong tonight.

He just looked at me without saying a word, his gaze really intense. I could tell he wasn't used to resistance from girls.

Finally, he asked, "What's wrong?"

"Nothing is wrong," I said. I scooted over toward him on the sofa and put my hand on his hand. We just stared at each other.

He cracked a smile, like he knew something I didn't. "You must be worried about Jay."

"I told you Jay is not my boyfriend, we're just going to the dance together."

"So you decided to go to the dance with him after all?"

"Yeah, well you said you wouldn't be caught dead at the dance."

"And I wouldn't. Nothing has changed," he said, then he put his hand behind my head bringing my face close to his. Our lips locked. He was a good kisser, but our rhythm was off. His teeth crashed into my lip. I whispered, "Slow down, babe."

Just then Candace bolted in the room, screaming. "I want you to make that faggot get out of my house, DeMarco."

DeMarco and I stood up from the sofa and stared at Candace. Her hair was disheveled and her blouse was unbuttoned. Tears rolled down her cheek. I ran to her side and put my arms around

158

"He tried to rape me."

"What?" DeMarco said.

"Yeah, we were in the basement and he grabbed my booty and I told him to stop then. He grabbed me around the waist and pulled me toward him. Forced me to kiss him and threw me on the floor and ripped my blouse off. He kept saying, 'Shorty, you know you want it.'"

Jimmy appeared, laughing as he held his pants up. "She's lying. Didn't nobody do all of that. Besides, she kept bending over like she wanted it. Trust me, bro, I know when somebody wants it and she wanted it. She was teasing me."

"Did I say I wanted you?"

"You didn't have to, shorty. Look at what you got on. Why are you wearing those tight jeans, if you don't want me to look at you."

"Look but don't touch."

"You tripping, shorty, we take you out for a spin and show you a good time and I don't get no goods. What part of the game is that?"

It was time for me to step in. "This ain't no game. This is real life. That's your problem—you think everything is a game, Jimmy," I said. I felt obligated at that point to say something. Felt obligated to protect my friend. "Jimmy, you've done nothing but brought negative energy here all night."

Kevin Elliott

"Get this dude outta my house, I don't want to see him again."

DeMarco walked over to Jimmy. I guess he wanted to hear Jimmy's version of the story. I didn't care about his version. Candace was my friend and I believed her. As far as I was concerned her version was the only version.

He pulled Jimmy aside, and it looked as if he didn't want us to hear what he had to tell Jimmy.

But we did. Jimmy shouted, "That broad is lying, DeMarco. She just kept bending over, she wanted me to push up on her."

"Dude, I bent over to straighten up the magazines," Candace said.

"Oh, yeah right like straightening some damn magazines was that important, you wanted me to notice you, I saw how you were looking at me."

"Get this dude outta my house. As a matter of fact, both of you D Boys get outta my house."

Dang, I wished Candace hadn't have called them D Boys. Though we both knew DeMarco was a drug dealer, I didn't want him to think that's what I felt about him. Calling them D Boys gave me away.

DeMarco glanced at me and then looked at Jimmy. Then he stared at Candace. His expression said that Candace had messed up his night. But I was still on Candace's side.

Finally, I said, "DeMarco, I think you and Jimmy should leave. I will call you later, but really I think you should go." I could see that DeMarco wanted to get something off his chest. I just hoped the situation wasn't going to escalate.

"Wassup with your friend just talking to me any kind of way?"

"What did I say that was so wrong, DeMarco? I called you a D Boy. So you're saying that you're not a drug dealer?"

"Listen, you don't know what I do." DeMarco stared at her. He looked as if he wanted to slap her, but I hope he knew that was *not* going to happen. He turned to me and said, "Listen, I'm really sorry, shorty."

Jimmy butted in with "Sorry for what? We ain't do shit to be sorry about."

DeMarco grabbed Jimmy's arm and led him to the door. Jimmy fumbled with his belt and zipped his pants up. This dude was indeed scum as far as I was concerned. I didn't ever want to see him again.

Before DeMarco closed the door, he glanced back at me and said, "I'm gonna call you later. Maybe we can hook up."

"Maybe," I said as I held Candace. I'd have to calm my girl down before I made plans to meet up with him.

Candace had a lot to say about Jimmy, but after about an hour I was able to break free from her and head on out. Candace let me borrow her car so I could get home, so I texted DeMarco to meet me at the entrance of Candace's neighborhood. I followed him to an apartment on the other side of town. It was a very nice apartment, but plain. It was decorated in white leather furniture, and there were no pictures on the walls. I could tell it was a guy's apartment.

"So whose place is this?" I asked

"It's my brother's," he said.

"The same brother that let you drive his truck."

"Yeah."

Now I was kind of nervous and wondered if there were drugs stashed in the place. The last thing I needed was to go be hauled off to jail. My mom would kill me. My mind began to race. This had to be some sort of stash house, or else there would be pictures. This place didn't even look like it was lived in.

"He knows you're here?"

"I got the key, don't I?"

I smiled at his sarcasm and tried to relax a bit. If I didn't calm down, I'd talk myself into leaving. And after a night like this, DeMarco would probably write me off as high strung.

We sat on the couch and he said, "I'm sorry for how Jimmy treated your friend."

"It's okay I don't hold that against you, I know you didn't have nothing to do with how he was acting."

"No, it's not okay, and I told him that he shouldn't have done that, told him he could have us both locked up."

He sounded sincere. Maybe he was sorry.

Our eyes met and held.

He put his arm around me. "Shorty, I want you to be my girl."

"Where did that come from?"

"My heart." He pointed to his chest.

Ahhh. I thought he looked so cute and I believed him

He kissed me and grabbed my booty. *Dang,* I thought. *He was trying to see my blue thong tonight.* I didn't know if I could resist.

# 4

Candace called the next day and the first thing she said was, "I can't believe you hooked up with DeMarco."

"Why not?"

"Him and his boy are so dang trifling and disrespectful."

"What are you talking about? DeMarco didn't do anything to you."

"Yeah, but he acted like he believed what Jimmy was telling him."

I stared at my phone. I really wanted to hang up on her. Who was she to tell me who I could hang out with. I understood why she would be upset. I was there, and I was upset with her. I wished that what happened wouldn't have ever happened, but it did and there was nothing I could do to change it.

"So you're gonna pick a dude over your best friend? That dude hasn't been there for you since the second grade. I was there for you when your parents divorced."

Now one thing I hate is when somebody does something for me or is supportive of me in a certain way and then brings it up. Candace was pissing me off.

"Candace, what is your point?"

"My point is we're in high school. There will be more boyfriends, but you only have one best friend."

"Okay . . ."

"This dude is bad news, I told you that before, you need to leave him alone."

"You need to stay out of my business."

"Zori, I'm just being a concerned friend. There is nothing wrong with me being concerned."

"A friend? Is that what you call being a friend." I put the phone down for a second, trying to gather my thoughts and keep my composure. I didn't want to curse my best friend out, but she was making me so mad. I picked the phone up again. "Listen, Candace, I'm not going to stop seeing DeMarco for something he had nothing to do with."

"O.M.G. He had nothing to do with? You must have forgotten. He was the one that invited Jimmy to come with us in the first place. It was DeMarco's idea. It was DeMarco's friend."

"Okay, but he apologized. What else do you want me to do?"

"You need to stop seeing him."

"You're crazy."

"No you're crazy, you're the one with the thug boyfriend."

"Listen Candace, just because he didn't come from a nice neighborhood like us don't mean that he's bad."

"Neighborhood has nothing to do with him being a thug, he's a thug because he sells drugs."

"You don't know that."

"Duh . . . You know he sells drugs, now what if we would have gotten pulled over with that weed on us."

"We didn't, Candace."

"I know we didn't, but we could have."

She was being ridiculous and argumentative, I didn't want to keep arguing with her. I knew she was talking like this because she was upset and she was clearly trying to make me feel guilty about what happened, but that was not my fault. There was an awkward silence on the phone.

Candace finally said, "You should not be with him."

"Why?"

"Because he's a hoodlum and a drug dealer."

"That's not all true, and even if it was, it wouldn't stop me."

"I'm telling your mom."

Now this chick was being ridiculous. How was she gonna tell on me. Why was she going to tell

on me. I knew so many of her secrets. "You remember Barry the college boy, don't you?"

Barry was a senior at the University of North Carolina. And Candace had gone out with him several times. He took her virginity. She would still see him from time to time and I'm sure they were still sleeping together.

Again there was silence on the phone. She was thinking. I knew she was trying to decide if her information was worth sharing. While I knew my Mom would be pissed at me and probably take my car away, her Dad would go ballistic. He thought she was still a virgin.

"Fine then, just don't speak to me anymore," she said.

I hung up the phone.

Three days later, I was still mad about my conversation with Candace. But as I sat with DeMarco in his brother's truck, waiting for classes to start, I knew I'd made the right decision. He held me tight and kissed me softly. Then he whispered, "I really wanna be with you."

As much as I wanted to hear those words from him, I wondered what he meant. I really liked him but I didn't know if there was more to it than my fascination with being with a bad boy.

Luckily, I didn't get a chance to answer 'cause a

phone buzzed and it wasn't mine. I always kept my phone off at school 'cause we weren't allowed to have our phones on. "I think your phone is ringing."

DeMarco didn't move an inch toward his phone; he just kept kissing my neck. And at that moment I wanted to leave school. I wanted it to be just him and me. But the buzzing of his phone interrupted my thoughts.

I spotted his bag in the backseat of the car. The buzzing noise came from the book bag. I grabbed it.

He yanked my arm hard. "Gimme my book bag."

Oh no he didn't try to snatch that bag from me. His D Boy was showing.

We tussled until he finally gained possession of the bag. Just then, the bag opened and the phone—and four bags of marijuana—spilled from the book bag.

A hardened look appeared on his face. He scooped the baggies up and placed them back in the book bag. "Yo, get out of this car."

"What?" I knew I'd heard him right. But it startled me a little.

"Get out, now."

"I won't." I crossed my arms and refused to move.

"Why do you have to be so nosey?"

"Why you gotta be a drug dealer?"

"Drugs? Who got drugs? This ain't nothing; this is weed."

My face became stern. "You can go to jail for this."

"I ain't afraid of jail."

"Well, I am. I got my whole life ahead of me and there is no way that I'm going to jail for you or nobody else."

I uncrossed my arms and looked at my watch. It was almost time for us to go to class. "Well, then, you're stupid. And I don't wanna be with a stupid guy."

He dropped his head. Looked down at the floor. There was a brief silence as he gathered his thoughts and I gathered mine. It was funny that what had drawn me to him—that bad boy image— had also turned me off. I guess I liked the fact that he was a bad boy until I actually saw the drugs. Seeing those bags of weed changed the way I felt about him. The way I felt about the whole bad boy persona. I still liked him, but I knew it was like mom said: People won't change because I want them to change. They will change when they want to change.

He looked at me with sad eyes. "Hey, I'm sorry."

"Look, I just don't want you to go to jail, because this is something you don't have to do."

"You don't know what I have to do. You have your mother."

"And you're a gifted athlete that takes advanced classes."

"I don't need you to give me a speech."

I could see he was going to stand his ground on this, so I opened the door of the car and got out. "See you later."

"Later, shorty."

I was on my way to my homeroom when Jay appeared. "Can I speak to you for a minute?" His voice was businesslike. Not friendly at all.

I looked at my watch. I was going to be late for homeroom. So was he. "Can it wait till after homeroom? I will meet you in front of C building."

"It won't take long."

"Okay." I studied his face. Why wasn't he smiling? This is not what I was used to with Jay.

"Are you DeMarco's girlfriend?"

My mind raced. Why did Jay ask me this? Where had he gotten this information from? Though I wasn't officially DeMarco's girlfriend, I felt like I'd been caught.

"Jay, where is this coming from?"

"Yes or no?" he said. His voice still stern like Mr. Addison the principal.

"No."

"Okay, I saw a picture of you and him."

"A picture of me and him?" I thought back. Then I remembered the picture that DeMarco and I had taken the night of the double date.

"Okay, we went out before and we'd taken a picture. I am in high school as you are in high school, I have to focus on my work, as you should. I have no time for boyfriends, but I do date. Jay, I don't owe you an explanation."

"You're absolutely right, I just don't want to be caught up in the middle of no B.S. I've known DeMarco since we were little and he's a pretty tough dude."

Wow, Jay sounded like such a wus. "Look, Jay, I'll say it again. I don't owe you no explanation and I don't belong to DeMarco."

"I'm sorry, I just wanted to know. Wanted to know if I had to watch my back or something. I know how some guys can get over girls."

"There is no need to be sorry, Jay. Like I said before, I don't belong to anyone. Not you. Not DeMarco."

"But does he know that?"

I was a bit annoyed at that point. The warning bell rang and I didn't have all day to be explaining to Jay that me and DeMarco were not an item, I'd just told him that I didn't belong to him or nobody else. What was so hard about that to understand? Why didn't Jay get that. For somebody that was so intelligent, he really lacked common sense. He didn't even have a spoonful. "Jay, I'm not DeMarco's girlfriend."

"I understand."

"Anything else you would like to know?"

He smiled. "I'm ready for the dance."

"I'm ready for class." I looked at my watch. The bell rang.

"I gotta go Jay."

* * *

After school, DeMarco called and told me to meet him at Southpark Mall. I met him at the entrance of the mall. He said that he wanted to take me shopping. No guy had ever taken me shopping, except my dad. At first I was kind of hesitant about going shopping with him, I didn't want him to think I owed him anything and darn sure didn't want him to think that I could be bought. But all my reservations went out the window when we walked into the Abercrombie and Fitch store and I saw these distressed jeans that I had to have and when I went to the Gap store I saw two belts that I wanted. I got two pairs of shoes from Aldo's and a couple of dresses from Betsy Johnson. I know DeMarco had to have spent at least seven hundred dollars, maybe more. Every time he pulled a wad of money from his pocket, I would look away. Even though we're just buying clothes I just felt like what we were doing was wrong, and it didn't help that people stared at us probably wondering where in the heck were these kids getting all this cash. He carried my bags and when we walked out of the mall I said, "Thanks."

He just looked at me for a long time, as if he wanted to tell me something. I wanted to ask him why he was doing this. I wanted to ask him where he'd gotten the money to pay for everything we'd bought today, but I knew that would be a stupid question, because I'd just seen the weed he'd brought to school to sell. I knew that he'd bought me these things with his drug money. I looked down at the shopping bags, trying not to think about where he'd gotten the money to buy me these nice things. I knew that I would have to hide my new stuff from my mom, 'cause she'd want to know how I came by it and I didn't want to have a conversation with her about DeMarco and his drug dealing.

DeMarco put his arms around me and said, "I love you, baby."

And I believed him.

# 5

The next day, I was on my way to school when my phone rang. It was Daddy, I hadn't heard from him in two weeks. He had been sent to New Jersey by his job. I answered on the first ring. "Hey, Daddy."

"Hey, how has my girl been?"

"I've been good. I missed you."

"Well, that's exactly why I called you to let you know that I'll be in town later this evening. I want to meet up with you and maybe we can go get something to eat, and I want to take you to the mall, you know take you shopping."

Wow, I thought, I just gone shopping with DeMarco and now Daddy was going to take me shopping. This was perfect. This way if Mom ever came in my room and questioned the things that DeMarco bought me, I could just say Daddy bought them. She wouldn't question him. She knows he buys me things all the time.

"I can't wait, Daddy!"

"I can't wait to see my little girl."

I hate being addressed as a little girl, but somehow when Daddy called me his little girl, it always made me feel special like I was cared for and protected, the same feeling I had gotten yesterday with DeMarco in the mall.

The next morning, I dressed for school in the new Abercrombie distressed jeans that I had gotten yesterday. I ordinarily wouldn't have worn them this soon after buying them, but it was a perfect time to wear them. Mom had left for work when I woke up and I knew she wouldn't get off till six o'clock, so there was no way she would see me with them on. I would have taken them off by the time she got off work. I saw DeMarco in the parking lot sitting in the truck with Lil Jimmy. I was actually hoping that they didn't see me. I knew they were probably smoking or something. Or there was probably a few bags of weed in the truck. Either way I didn't want to be involved in whatever they had going on. I kept walking. I would see DeMarco some other time.

Lil Jimmy yelled out, "Shorty."

I turned and he said, "How you gonna walk past us? You see us over here."

I might as well get them out the way. I approached the truck and just as I suspected, a strong marijuana stench seeped through the windows. DeMarco's eyes were almost closed.

"Hey baby," he said.

"Hey, I guess y'all ain't going to class, huh?"

DeMarco looked down at his watch. "Debating it right now."

Jimmy turned to DeMarco and said. "Man, let's just go home, let's get outta here before one of these snitches spots us."

I made eye contact with DeMarco. "Don't listen to your friend, you need to come on to class."

Jimmy looked at me. He was clearly upset with what I had said. "Now, shorty, you need to stay out of this."

"Jimmy, your energy is negative."

Jimmy looked at DeMarco and then back at me and then said "You need to check this broad."

I was upset now, because I did *not* like anyone calling me a broad. I swear I have never fought a boy but if Jimmy called me out of my name one more time I was gonna punch this little munchkin in his face. "Jimmy, don't call me out of my name again. I didn't call you out of your name, so please don't call me outta my name again."

"You tripping. How you gonna say Jimmy is negative energy but I can't say nothing to you."

"I just notice when DeMarco is around you, he's smoking and debating skipping school. And you're just so freaking disrespectful."

"Now how are you gonna call me disrespectful, when you're the one that was trying to walk by without speaking after my man took you to the mall and splurged on little bourgie self."

I couldn't believe what I had just heard. It was obvious DeMarco had bragged to his friends that he had taken me shopping. Like I was in need or something. I didn't ask him to take me shopping and I wasn't about to let his friend talk to me like I was some low budget hood rat.

"What is he talking about?" I asked DeMarco, though it was obvious that he was talking about our little trip to the mall.

DeMarco's eyes had been almost shut but at my tone, his eyes were wide open. I had his full attention. He looked at Jimmy. "He don't know what he's talking about."

"He just said that you took me shopping."

"I told him we went to the mall."

I was infuriated now. This dude Jimmy must have thought I was a charity case and DeMarco must have thought I could be bought with a few items at the mall.

DeMarco got out of his truck and approached me, wrapping his arms around me. "Listen babe I'm sorry about Jimmy."

"How many times are you going to be sorry? I swear to you one of these days that dude is gonna get you in big trouble."

DeMarco looked at me as he held me. His eyes looked very sad, he said. "You don't understand he's like a brother to me."

I looked at my watch and said, "I have to go to class and you should too."

I was so glad to see my daddy's car in the driveway when I came home from school. He was smiling brightly when he saw me. He looked magnificent today. Daddy was always a good looking man but he looked extra fit today. I knew he'd been working out a lot lately and it showed. Daddy was fifty but if it wasn't for the few strands of gray hair in his goatee, Daddy wouldn't look a day over thirty-eight. He gave me a warm hug. "I missed you so much, sunshine."

"I missed you, too."

I ran in the house and put up my book bag and came back and jumped in Daddy's car.

He said, "Let's go pick up Candace."

I kind of figured he would want to go pick up Candace or at least ask about her. Both my parents had known Candace since she was a baby, and Candace and I were like sisters even though Candace had a sister that was ten years older than she was. She and I were closer since we were the same age. I didn't want to tell Dad that we weren't speaking, but I knew he was going to insist we go pick her up. "Daddy, Candace and I aren't speaking."

"Why not?"

"We had a disagreement."

He kept driving. He seemed lost in thought,

probably trying to figure out a way to get the information out of me without prying. I knew I could trust Daddy with more information than I gave Mom, so I might as well spill the beans. This awkward silence was killing me. "Candace got mad at me because we'd gone out on a double date and the guy that she was with tried to force himself on her."

"Wait a minute, that doesn't make any sense, why would she be mad at you? You didn't have anything to do with it. Did you?"

"Of course not, you know me better than that."

He smiled. "I know I raised you better than that."

"So how long has it been since you spoke to her last?"

"It's been a few days."

"I think you should apologize. Even though it wasn't your fault you should be the bigger person."

"I did apologize."

"And she's still not speaking to you?" He looked confused. So I decided that I would tell him a little bit more of the story so he could get a better idea, but I couldn't tell him the whole story because God only knew what would happen to me if I'd told him that DeMarco was a hustler.

"Candace wants me to stop seeing the boy that I was with that night."

"Why?"

"Well she thinks he's bad news."

Dad looked at me suspiciously and I said, "Before you make assumptions, Candace is basing this solely on his friend's behavior. I mean she thinks DeMarco is a hoodlum just because of the way his friend Jimmy is."

"So Candace isn't being fair," he said, then he looked at me. "Unless you're not telling the whole story."

"Well, DeMarco is from a pretty rough neighborhood."

He smiled. "Well I'm from the hood and so is your mother. Can't hold that against him."

"Exactly." I smiled. "See, Candace believes that if you didn't come from a good home like hers, that you're probably no good."

"Really?" Dad said. "Well, that's surprising. Her Mom and Dad are the most down to earth people I've ever met."

"I know and that's what's surprising when she acts so uppity."

"Well, I think you need to make up with her, you guys have been friends too long to let some boy come in between you two."

We finally arrived at the mall. I led us to Abercrombie and Fitch and Forever21 before heading to Nordstrom's, where I got some Uggs. After we finished shopping we went to the Cheesecake Factory and got some Dulce De Leche cheesecake and headed home.

When we got home, I gave Dad a big hug and kiss and walked in the house. Mom was sitting on the sofa watching the news. She looked up. "Was that your Dad that dropped you off?"

"Yeah, he called me yesterday to let me know that he was going to take me shopping."

"That was nice of him."

I smiled. "Yeah, I really needed some new things."

"You know you got too many clothes as it is."

"Mom, wasn't it you who said that a girl could never have too many clothes?"

She laughed. "I did say that, didn't I?"

"Yes, you did!"

"So where did you get those jeans that you're wearing?"

Dang, I had totally forgotten to take these jeans off. My plans were to take them off before Mom got home from work, but I had forgot all about taking them off when I saw Dad waiting to take me shopping. I couldn't tell her that they were Candace's because we weren't speaking. Even if we were, she wouldn't believe me anyway, because we aren't the same size. I froze for a second with no explanation.

"Where did you get those jeans?"

"Abercrombie and Fitch." I said, not quite giving her the answer she wanted. "Dad bought them and I wore them out of the store."

"Why?"

"Because I always wanted a pair of distressed jeans."

"That's why you have a pair of jeans like that.

Remember, I bought you some from the Gap last year."

I had totally forgotten about those jeans. But I wasn't caught in a lie just yet. "Yeah, but they are too small now."

"That doesn't explain why you left out of the store with these jeans on."

"I just wanted to wear them out, Mom. No big deal."

She took a deep breath and she looked like she was frustrated with something. Somebody. Me. "You're right, it really wouldn't be a big deal if it wasn't a lie."

"What are you talking about?"

"Talking about going in your room and finding the receipt for those distressed jeans, along with two pair of shoes, and some other things. All paid with cash. All purchased yesterday."

The room closed in on me and I wanted to run, but I couldn't. Mom's face got angrier. She had caught me in two lies.

"Where did you get the money to buy this stuff?"

I sat on the recliner and looked Mom in the eye. I decided not to make the situation worse and decided to steer a little closer to the truth. "This boy from school named DeMarco."

"Who is DeMarco and where did he get this kind of money? How old is this boy?"

"He's seventeen."

"Why is he buying you stuff? How can he afford this?"

181

SWAG

"His mom died and she left him some money." I actually didn't feel too bad for telling that lie because it was partly true. His mom had died, she just didn't leave him any money, but Mom didn't have to know that part. I absolutely could not let her know that DeMarco was a hustler. No way.

Mom held the receipts up. "This boy spent almost eight hundred dollars on you. What high school kid does that?"

"Mom, he's a nice guy."

"Listen, I don't care how nice he is. You're giving him all this stuff back. I want you to gather all this stuff up and return it to him."

"Why?"

"Because it's not yours. You didn't pay for it. You didn't earn it, and you are not for sale, young lady."

"I don't understand."

Mom's face became stern. "Anything that you need, me or your dad will get it for you. You're taking this stuff back to him and I don't want to hear nothing else about it."

"That's not fair!" I said, but I knew there was no point in arguing with her, I would take this stuff back to DeMarco tomorrow.

"How much are those jeans? I will write him a check for those jeans, since they've been worn."

"You're the one holding the receipts."

"Don't get smart with me."

I headed to my room and put my things up that Dad bought me.

Kevin Elliott

* * *

The next day at school, I handed DeMarco the bag with the things he bought me at the mall and a check for ninety dollars for the distressed jeans that I'd worn.

He said, "I don't understand what's going on, are you upset with what Lil Jimmy said?"

"Yes, but that's not the reason I'm giving this stuff back."

"Well, what's the reason?" He sounded confused. He tried to hand it back to me but I wouldn't take it back.

"Mom found out that you took me to the mall."

"So what's the problem?"

Wow. I couldn't believe he was really confused. I guess in his world taking little hood rats shopping was common. I would have to explain to him why I couldn't accept this stuff without hurting his feelings. Without him thinking that I was too uppity to take the things he bought me and I really didn't want him to think that I didn't appreciate it.

"Listen, Mom thinks you're trying to buy me."

He laughed out loud. "Nobody is trying to buy you, I was just simply being nice to the girl I like."

I looked him directly in his face. He looked sincere. "At first I argued with her about it, but I have to admit that this is not right. I cannot accept these things, because I didn't pay for them."

"I see, your mom sees something wrong with a guy buying a girl he likes gifts."

I took a deep breath. I was actually tired of explaining to him why this was wrong on so many levels. "DeMarco we're in high school. Not in college, we're kids."

"I see."

"And she wanted to know how you got that kind of money to buy this stuff."

"What did you tell her?"

"I told her your mother died and left you the money."

He laughed again. "You were quick on your feet."

"It was a lie, and I don't want to be a liar."

"Okay, I guess I'll go put this stuff in my brother's truck and I'll take it back to the mall later."

I gave him a hug and watched him walk away.

# 6

_____

I was sitting in the cafeteria by myself, since Candace and I still weren't speaking. This was the part that really sucked about falling out with your best friend. Not that I needed someone to eat with me, but I really missed her company. I wondered if she missed mine. After I had finished my food and was about to go put my tray up, Malaka came running to the table. "I need to show you something. Hurry up."

I put my tray up in a hurry, wondering what it was that she wanted to show me and why it was so urgent. As soon as we walked outside she pointed and I knew exactly what the sense of urgency was all about. I saw DeMarco with his arms around Christian Byers. Christian was a very cute girl that I've known since I was six. We'd taken gymnastics together and we were on the same ninth grade cheerleading team. I wouldn't call her a friend but we weren't enemies.

I walked up to the two lovebirds.

"Hey, DeMarco."

He looked stunned. He removed his arm from around her.

"Hey, Zori," Christian said.

"Hi, how are you Christian?"

"Good." She looked at DeMarco "What's going on here?" she asked sensing the tension.

"That's what I would like to know," I asked.

Christian looked at me and then back at DeMarco. "Is Zori your girlfriend?"

"No, I don't have a girlfriend," he said.

"No, DeMarco is not my boyfriend but we've been seeing each other. Right, DeMarco?"

Christian made eye contact with me. "Hey, listen, Zori I don't want any problems, I didn't know y'all were seeing each other." Her voice sounded sincere and Christian was not the kind of girl that would lie for no reason.

She said to DeMarco. "Goodbye, DeMarco, and lose my number, will you?"

When she was gone, I said, "I can't believe you tried to play me like that."

"Listen, shorty, I never said you and I were a couple."

He was right and I knew that I had been talking to other guys. So really I didn't have too much that I could say, but he did lead me on.

"And you're going to that stupid ass dance with Jay. So what are you talking about?"

"You know I'm going with Jay beause you won't take me. But for real, you said you loved me. Did you say that to hear yourself talk or were you serious?"

He looked away which led me to believe that he was just talking to hear himself talk. Then he said, "Every time I told you I loved you, you never said anything back. Not once, you never answered and now you're letting your mom run your life, telling you that you cannot accept gifts from me."

"Hey, I'm in high school, my mom is supposed to run my life."

He looked away from me and made eye contact with Malaka who was standing beside me, popping gum. "So you're the one that ratted on me."

What? I couldn't believe him. He had some nerve trying to blame Malaka for him getting caught.

"You leave her alone," I said.

"Trust me. Looking the way she looks, she will be left alone."

"Dude, you're a loser," Malaka said, then walked away.

"Why were you being mean to her?"

"Because I know she was the one that told you that I was out here with Christian. I saw her walk by and then all of a sudden she's out here with you."

"What difference does it make?" I asked. Knowing he was trying to divert the attention away from him.

"It makes no difference at all. Like I said before, you're going to the dance with Jay, so how can you talk about me."

"The difference between me and you was that you knew I was talking to Jay. I didn't know you were talking to Christian."

"You never asked me whether I was talking to other girls."

Now I know this dude wasn't serious. He thinks I'm some air headed bimbo, but rather than argue with him, I said, "You're right," and I walked away before I let my emotions get the most of me.

# 7

Time flew quickly after that. Before I knew it, it was time for the Christmas dance, and my mom was more excited about it than I was. I definitely liked my dress; it was a mint green color with a high waist and a tight fit that celebrated my lean body. Mom held the camera smiling. She'd always lived vicariously through me. My mom had lived a rough life in the country. She'd been raised by her father. Her mom had died early of cancer. They were very poor. Her dad worked hard but he was an alcoholic. So she didn't get to go to dances. She never went to the prom. Her first boyfriend came when she was twenty-two. Mom took pictures of me in the kitchen where the lighting was good. She set the timer on the camera and we took several together.

An hour later a yellow stretch Hummer pulled

up in front of the house. A chauffeur opened the door and Jay appeared. Me and Mom looked at him through the window. I had to admit he looked handsome, very handsome. Mom opened the door and greeted Jay with a hug. "Hello, Jay."

"Hey, Ms. Neal."

Jay's eyes met mine and they traveled my body. When they got to my waist they lingered for a while. I smiled. He smiled. He looked at me like I was a delicious steak and I liked that feeling. "Come, come to the kitchen," Mom said.

We went into the kitchen. Mom took more pictures. Jay held my waist tight and I have to admit I liked the way it felt. Magical, for the first time I felt in sync with Jay.

After about twenty pictures, I said, "Mom we gotta be going."

"Oh, yeah right." She said as she walked us out to the Hummer.

The back of the Hummer was huge and very luxurious with a bar. There was champagne, I grabbed a bottle and looked at the label. It was the good stuff.

Jay said, "Open it, let's take a drink."

"You're a drinker?"

"No, are you?"

"No, but it's a big night."

I looked up at the driver. He wasn't looking in the mirror, I didn't think he could see us at all. I knew that the limo company and driver knew we were underage. Why did they have the alcohol so accessible? I had never drunk champagne before, but I felt tempted to take a sip.

Jay grabbed the bottle, got the cork-screw, popped the champagne bottle, and poured me a glass. I sipped it slow. Jay found mini liquor bottles. He opened a bottle of Absolut and tried to drink it straight up before spitting it out.

I laughed at him.

"This stuff is strong."

"Try the champagne."

He poured himself a glass.

We sipped the champagne together. He scooted over next to me and placed his arm around me. I'd never really looked at Jay, but tonight I realized he had really nice arms. They were so big and strong I felt so protected, so secure. His phone buzzed, interrupting my thoughts.

He looked down at this phone. "It's my boy Kevin, wanting to know where we're at."

His boy texted him. I wanted somebody to text. I wanted to text Candace, but she was still mad at me and I really missed her. We would still be speaking if I'd been talking to Jay instead of DeMarco.

Two glasses later, we were at the hotel where the dance was. I was a little buzzed but I felt amazing.

When we stepped inside the ball room, all eyes were on us. I saw Candace with this guy Michael Finely. She looked great and they made a good couple. She nodded but she didn't speak. Jay's friend Kevin came over with this Latina, Adrianna. I forgot her last name but we were in Chemistry class together. She was a pretty girl with long blond hair and lips like a black girl and she had braces. She'd worn them for a while, so long that I knew that it had to be time for them to come off soon.

With a big smile, she said, "You look great."

She looked great as well wearing a gold dress that flowed freely at the bottom.

I nodded at Kevin, and he gave me a hug. When we were done with our hellos, Adrianna pulled my arm. "We're going to the little girls room," she announced to the boys.

Once inside the bathroom, she asked, "What y'all got planned after the dance?"

I was having fun so far, but I wasn't sure about hanging out with Jay after the dance. I didn't want him to get the wrong idea. So I said, "I'm going home."

She opened her white clutch and showed me two mini bottles of liquor. My mind went back to the back of the limo, and wondered if I was on a slippery slope with the liquor.

"You drink?" I asked, surprised. This girl struck me as a nerd, but then again so did Jay, and he'd taken a drink tonight.

"Sometimes. Do you?"

"I did tonight." I smiled

She went into one of the stalls and popped open a bottle of Tanqueray and drank it all.

She handed me a mini bottle of Scotch, I was already buzzing from the champagne but I drank it all.

"Y'all should come with us tonight."

"Where to?"

She smiled, her breath reeking of the liquor. I'm sure mine was too at this time. Eww, I needed to catch up with a breath mint.

"Kevin got a room at the Marriott near South Park Mall."

"A room?" I think I was about to get more information than I needed.

"A suite!" she said, her eyes bulging. She reached in the clutch again and pulled out a pack of Altoid chewing gum and passed me several pieces.

A room? I didn't want to go to a room with Jay. Didn't want to put myself in that position. Because clearly this Adrianna girl was ready to do whatever Kevin wanted her to do with him and I was not at that place with Jay.

"I'm going home."

"You know Jay really likes you."

I smiled but didn't say anything.

"I mean he rented that Hummer and everything. Not many guys would do that."

I hoped this heifer wasn't insinuating that just because Jay had rented a Hummer that I owed him something because I didn't owe him a thing.

"I like Jay, too."

"But you're not going to the room with us?"

"Listen, Jay and I didn't discuss no room."

My phone buzzed. It was a text from Candace.

So Adrianna is your new best friend. How fast we move on.

I texted her back.

Whatever

When Adrianna and I stepped out of the bathroom, I saw Candace and two other girls standing nearby. As we passed them Candace rolled her eyes.

When we reached Jay and Kevin, Jay said, "I saw your girl Candace."

"Did she speak?"

"Yeah, why?" He looked confused.

"Oh, nothing . . . Nothing at all."

"You guys are still friends aren't you?"

"Yes," I lied. I didn't want to talk about it.

Adrianna put her arms around Kevin. An edited version of Gucci Mane's song was playing. All the music was edited, the radio version, but most of us had heard the explicit versions. I was sure many of the staff and chaperones had not.

Jay held my hand and said, "I'm really glad you came."

I smiled and he smiled. I was a little light-headed. Still thinking about Candace. I really missed her. I looked past him to where Candace stood across the room and we made eye contact. She looked away.

My phone buzzed again. Text from DeMarco.

I got a room in the hotel, room 322. Come up after the dance.

I don't know why, but a part of me wanted to go see him after the dance. This would be entirely disrespectful to Jay, and my mom would kill me if she knew. But wait! Why did DeMarco get the room? How did he get the room? He's underage but maybe that doesn't mean anything anymore. Kevin got a room across town.

Smitty featuring Rick Ross came on. *Died In Your Arms Tonight.* I love that song, so I led Jay to the dance floor. I felt so good, so liberated. Music does that for me, especially songs I like. Adrianna and Kevin danced next to us. Adrianna moved closer to me, sandwiching me to Jay.

Mr. Patterson, the assistant principal, was suddenly at our side. "Ladies, you're dancing too close."

We both backed away, laughing. I had to admit I was having fun, more fun than I'd had in a long time. I felt different; maybe it was the alcohol. Now I wanted some more.

"Adrianna, come with me to the bathroom."

Once inside the restroom, "Do you have any more liquor?"

Her eyes lit up. "Yes."

She dug into her clutch again and handed me a mini bottle of Ciroc.

"This is the last one."

"I don't wanna take your last."

"No, it's the last one in my clutch. Kevin and I have more in the car."

"Okay, great." I downed it with one swallow. It burned on the way down.

My phone buzzed. It was another text from DeMarco.

Are you coming to see me or not?

I text back: Maybe

DeMarco: I need to know

Me: Why? So if I don't come you can call one of your other girls?

DeMarco: You tripping

Me: You miss me?

DeMarco: I love you.

He loves me? Whatever. I hope he don't expect me to believe that. I know he doesn't love me, but I am tempted to go up to that room, just to see what kind of seduction he thinks would work on me. Hmmm . . .

"Who's texting you like that?" Adrianna asked.

"My mom," I lied.

"Yeah, my mom has texted me a few times to-night, too."

Adrianna passed me two pieces of gum.

"Thank you," I said. I decided I wanted to go see DeMarco.

When we stepped outside the restroom, I saw Candace again with her date. I attempted to walk past her, but she grabbed my arm. "Can we talk?"

I turned to face her and before either of us could say anything we embraced.

"I missed you," she said. She held me tight, I could feel her heart beat. I really missed her, too.

When we released each other, she said, "Zori, you've been drinking."

I blushed but didn't say anything. I thought the Altoid had covered it up, but apparently not.

Adrianna jumped in, confirming what I wanted to deny. "We got more in the car."

*Great, thanks!*

Candace gave Adrianna the stink eye. "No thank you, honey. I don't drink, I am underage."

I giggled. "It's a big night."

"A big night? This is a school dance. What's so big about it?" Candace asked.

"Don't you go and tell on me," I said. *Did I just slur my words?*

"Zori, I'm disappointed but I'm not going to tell on you."

"I'll see you before I leave," I said.

Candace looked at me like I disgusted her. "Okay."

Adrianna and I walked over to find Kevin and Jay talking to these two girls. One of them was Crystal Rose, the other one I had seen before but I didn't know her name. Crystal was an average looking girl. I could see why she was at the dance alone. The other girl was very pretty and Jay was talking to her. He was trying to play me out.

I stepped in between them. "Jay, can we talk?"

He was startled. He stepped around me and said," Excuse me," to the pretty girl.

She smiled and the look on her face said *I can have your man if I want to, but I don't want this bum.* I knew the look because I used the look often.

"What is wrong with you?" Jay asked.

"What is wrong with you is the question?" I said. Hands on my waist ready to go into combat.

"Have you been drinking?"

"You know I've been drinking, I've been drinking with you."

"Champagne yes, but we only had a little bit."

"Well, I've had some other liquor, too but I ain't drunk and that definitely don't give you the right to play me out."

"Nobody's playing you out. We're just having conversation."

"Yeah, but did you have to be all up in that girl's face? You came to the dance with me."

He put his arm around my waist and pulled me close and smiled. "Look who's jealous."

I freed myself from him. "Trust me, I ain't hardly jealous and if I was jealous it wouldn't be of that bum chick."

"I think you are," he said.

Adrianna came over and said, "Hope y'all can come with us tonight."

"Come where?" Jay asked.

"Kevin didn't tell you we got a room across town?"

Jay looked at me and asked, "Do you wanna go?"

"Not sure." I was being coy because now I had two invitations to weigh.

"I think we should go; it could be fun."

I hoped he didn't think that I was going to make out with him because he had rented a Hummer. I was not feeling him like that, so I was amazed that I was jealous that he was talking to that girl. My emotions had gotten the best of me. My emotions and the alcohol. I did like him, but now he probably thought that I liked him more than I actually did.

"I will get you home at a decent hour."

"Jay, I don't know about going to a room," I said.

Candace texted: Where y'all going after the dance?

Me: I don't know

The pretty girl came over and said, "Jay I will see you at school on Monday."

He smiled. His facial expression said he would devour her if he had a chance. He was really in tune with her. I wondered why he wanted me so much when it was obvious to me that he could have this girl if he wanted and she was very pretty. I think the fact that I didn't want him made him want me more. I rolled my eyes.

DeMarco texted: I need to see you.

I texted: I need to see you more.

I didn't even feel guilty anymore about wanting to be with DeMarco. Jay had a girl in the wings, and following after me was a waste of his time.

Kevin came over and pulled Jay aside. They looked in the direction of Crystal Rose and the pretty girl. They both were smiling. Adrianna seemed oblivious that Kevin and Jay were flirting right in our faces. I approached her. "I'm leaving."

"Why?" she asked.

With my hands on my waist, I said. "There is no way that I'm going to just stand here and let him flirt in my face. I'm not going to be disrespected by nobody."

Adrianna agreed. "I thought I was the only one that noticed this outright disrespect."

"You know I was just trying to be nice. Jay ain't even my type."

"I know. I didn't think y'all meshed well."

"Listen, I know you like Kevin, but what they're doing is wrong."

Adrianna's eyes became sad. "I know, and Kevin is always doing this kind of stuff. He is always being disrespectful, but now if you leave I'm leaving, but how are we going to leave? Where are we going?"

I hadn't planned on Adrianna leaving with me. I really didn't want anyone to know where I was going. I didn't want to tell her about the room that DeMarco had gotten but I had to at this point. I figured I could take her up to the room with me and then DeMarco and I could drop her off and come back to the room and chill.

"I have a friend who has a room here. We can go up and hang out with him for a while."

She smiled. "I'm cool with that."

Kevin and Jay were still looking at the pretty girl and Crystal Rose when we left the dance.

When DeMarco opened the door, the first person I saw was Lil Jimmy and I thought I was about to vomit. What in the world was he doing here? I thought I had explained to DeMarco that I couldn't stand this guy and yet he was in my presence again. He approached me with this stupid grin on his face. "Hey, shorty. So I see you decided to blow that stupid dance." His eyes grew big when he saw Adrianna. "Who is this little Mami?"

"I'm Adrianna." She grinned. Her braces gleamed. Jimmy was showing her more attention than Kevin had shown her the whole night.

"Well, I was just about to leave you two lovers alone but looks like there is somebody here for me." Jimmy said as he put his arm right around Adrianna's waist. She didn't seem to mind. She kept grinning.

"I'm Jimmy."

"Glad to meet you, Jimmy."

DeMarco whispered, "Ain't that Kev's girl-friend?"

"Yeah."

"What is she doing here?"

"Long story. I will tell you later. But in the meantime, let's pull those two apart. I don't think it's a good idea for Jimmy to try to talk to Adrianna."

"Why not?"

I thought back to the night when Jimmy tried to rape Candace but I didn't want to bring that up again. "Adrianna has a boyfriend."

"She's not acting like she has a boyfriend. Besides, Jimmy loves Hispanic girls."

What does that have to do with anything? He was acting like Hispanic girls were prettier than black girls or something. He kind of rubbed me the wrong way with that statement.

"Hey listen, I will make sure Jimmy is on his best behavior."

"Yeah, right. I wanna see you do that." I looked over at Jimmy who was holding a bottle of Ciroc in his hand.

"Jimmy, no drinking tonight," DeMarco said.

Jimmy turned to DeMarco and said, "Shorty has already been drinking."

DeMarco turned to me. "Is that right?"

Now everyone knows. "Yeah and I had a drink myself, there was alcohol in the limo."

He smiled, and his expression told me that he no longer thought of me as a goody two-shoes. I didn't know if that was good or bad. I put my arm around him. I was glad to have left the dance. I was glad to be with DeMarco, but a part of me wondered what Jay was doing. Was he looking for me? I began to feel guilty. I wondered how Adrianna was feeling about leaving Kevin, 'cause from the looks of it she wasn't even thinking about Kevin.

Jimmy and Adrianna went into the adjoining

room of the suite and closed the door. I didn't want to know what was going on behind that door. I just wanted to spend some time in De-Marco's arms. I took his hand and led him to the sofa. He smiled as I slipped off my shoes and curled up in his lap. Guess the alcohol was making me tired. Before I dozed off, I saw DeMarco reach for the television remote and turn on *Law & Order*.

My eyes couldn't have been closed more than ten minutes before I was awakened by a scream. Not again! DeMarco was asleep, so I nudged him and waved my hand at the door to the room where Adrianna and Jimmy went. DeMarco and I rose to our feet and walked into the bedroom and saw Adrianna in tears and Jimmy standing over her with his boxer shorts on.

"What's the matter, Adrianna?" I asked but I could clearly see what was wrong. Jimmy had tried to violate someone again. How come he can't get a girl to consent? Adrianna's hair was disheveled and her dress was ripped. Jimmy was obviously the kind of guy folks warned women and children about: a born sex offender.

"Get away from me," she said to Jimmy.

DeMarco sighed. "What happened now?"

Jimmy smiled, but to me it was a stupid grin. "Nothing. We were just kissing."

My flesh crawled.

"I-I-I, think he put something in my drink," Adrianna said. "All I know is I dozed and when I woke up he was on top of me trying to take my clothes off."

DeMarco yelled, "Jimmy, how can you be so dumb?"

"She's lying," Jimmy said, still looking stupid. Still with that dumb look on his face. The same look he had on his face the night he tried to take advantage of Candace.

"Get him away from me."

I ran to Adrianna's side. "It's okay, I'm here. I'm not going to let anything happen to you."

She looked at me and said, "I need to know his full name. He is not going to get away with this. I'm going to call the police on him tonight. He's going to jail. I'm going to make sure he doesn't do this to no other girl."

DeMarco looked panicked. He said, "No, you can't call the police on my friend, he didn't rape you." I know he didn't want his boy to get in trouble, but Jimmy did this to himself.

"I'm calling the police on both of y'all," Adrianna said as she pulled her BlackBerry from her purse.

I agree that was really foul what Jimmy had done to her but I swear I didn't want her to call the police. All I needed was my name involved with his in an attempted rape investigation. How would I explain to Mom what had happened? How would I explain why I was with DeMarco and not Jay? This night had turned out to be tragic.

Jimmy walked over toward DeMarco.

"Can y'all just leave out of the room for a moment?" I asked.

"I ain't going nowhere," Jimmy said. "I'm not going to allow somebody to call the police on me and lie. I'll call Kevin; I know he keeps you in line."

"I aint scared of Kev. He might be tall but I'll take a baseball bat to his dome."

"Leave the room." I pleaded with DeMarco.

He grabbed Jimmy by the arm and led him to the other room. When the door closed I said, "Look, Adrianna. I know you're upset and what Jimmy did was wrong, but you can't call the police."

She looked up at me, tears now coming down her face. I felt like crying when I saw her cry. Jimmy was indeed a creep, I don't know why I didn't just leave when I saw his face. I knew better; I knew he was bad news, and I felt some guilt in what had almost happened.

"That boy is a monster," she said.

"I know."

"Well, if you knew, why didn't you tell me he was a creep?"

"Look, I'm sorry, I'm really sorry this happened to you." I was about to cry. I fought hard to hold back my tears.

"You just don't understand how I feel. I feel so violated."

"I know, but calling the police ain't going to solve anything. It will cause more problems."

"He should be in jail."

"He didn't rape you."

"But he tried to."

"Listen, if you call the cops, I'm going to have a whole lot of explaining to do to my mom, and you're going to have to do a whole lot of explaining to your mom."

She looked at her dress. It was ripped, and I don't know how she was going to make it past her parents looking that way. If she's lucky, maybe they won't be waiting up for her.

"I can sew the dress," I said. "But please, I'm begging you not to call the police."

She sighed. "I won't call the police, but we're going to have to figure out how to fix the dress. I can't go home looking this way. My parents will call the cops themselves."

I let out a sigh of relief. "I can fix the dress. Don't you worry about that."

DeMarco took Jimmy home and went to CVS to buy a sewing kit. I stitched the dress up and with all the ruffles acting as camouflage, you couldn't tell the dress had been in pieces.

By the time I finished the dress Adrianna had calmed down and fixed her face. The night was still early, so I asked Adrianna to come along with me and DeMarco to the Waffle House to get something to eat. Adrianna was in good spirits and she was even laughing at some of DeMarco's jokes. We dropped her off at home at about 11 pm.

After that, me and DeMarco went to his brother's house and sat in the driveway and kissed. I didn't have much to say to him; so much had gone on that night, and I was still trying to figure out how things got out of hand. When he dropped me off at home, it was close to one in the morning, much later than I anticipated, so I hoped my mom wouldn't be up, looking for me.

When I eased in the door, I heard Mom snoring. Thank God she was asleep. I jumped in the shower; happy the night was over and even happier that Adrianna hadn't called the police.

Candace called the next day. I answered the phone on the first ring.

"Where did you go last night? Jay was looking all over for you."

"I left."

"That's obvious. Where did you go?"

"I was with DeMarco."

"O.M.G. You left the dance to be with DeMarco? Please tell me you are not serious."

"I did. What's the big deal?"

"The big deal is that you didn't go to the dance with DeMarco, you went with Jay. That was just plain out disrespectful."

"Jay is the one that was disrespectful to me." My mind went back to when Jay was talking to the pretty girl. Now, I really didn't care that Jay was talking to her, I just cared that he was doing it while he was my escort to the dance. He could talk to her on his own time. I wished I had not told her about DeMarco.

"Don't judge me," I said

"I'm just saying that is not right. Your mom didn't raise you to be like that. I know Jay is not your type but he is a nice guy, he didn't deserve that."

"I know, but he flirted with Crystal Rose's friend right in my face. I don't know her name, but you know who I'm talking about. That tall cute girl."

"Brittany."

"Yeah, I think Jay should talk to her. She's cute and I guess she's his type."

"Jay likes you and you know he likes you. He's always had a crush on you since the eighth grade."

"But he must like Brittany, too, I guess. I think Jay should be with her, they obviously have some kind of chemistry. Something that he and I don't have."

"So you left with DeMarco. I didn't see him at the dance and he doesn't strike me as the type of guy that would even be caught dead at a dance."

"He didn't go to the dance. He got a room in the hotel."

"So you planned to escape with him to the room?"

"No. I didn't know he had gotten a room in the

hotel. He texted me and told me he was in the room and that I should come up."

"So, he just assumed you would come to the room. Wow, he thinks highly of you."

We've been on good terms for less than a day, and Candace was already buggin' and grating on my nerves. "Listen, I told you the reason why I left. I don't want to talk about it anymore."

"Cool, let's not talk about it."

I heard a tap on my door. Before I could respond, Mom appeared in the doorway.

"What's up?"

"Jay is here and he looks upset about something. He wants to speak with you."

"Candace, I'll call you later."

Mom and I went into the kitchen where Jay waited. His face looked more hurt than angry as Mom had said. My heart skipped. "What's up?"

"That was really uncalled for, what you did to me last night."

Mom looked confused. Her gaze went from Jay's face to my face. Finally she asked. "What's wrong Jay? What happened?"

"I will let your daughter tell you."

"Somebody tell me something."

"Jay disrespected me at the dance last night. He flirted with this girl, Brittany right in my face."

Jay turned to Mom. "Ms. Neal, I ain't gonna lie. Brittany does like me, but I like Zori. I have always liked Zori and I did not disrespect her, she disrespected me."

"How did she disrespect you, Jay?" Mom asked with curious eyes.

I can't believe Jay is sitting here about to whine to my mom about what happened last night. About to tell on me. Now I would have to hear her mouth for days. She would not let me live this one down. I wished I could disappear right now. I wish I could make him disappear, or at least the hurt I caused him to disappear.

"She left the dance and went to be with another guy."

Mom turned to me, her face now red. I knew that look. I could tell she wanted to kill me. The last time I'd seen that look, I'd stolen her car and wrecked it. That happened when I was fourteen. For that I had gotten put on punishment for a month.

She asked, "Is this true?"

"I did leave the dance."

"With who?"

I didn't want to say I was with DeMarco. Mom had never met him and that would have made it worse. I didn't answer.

There was about a minute of silence before Jay said, "She was with DeMarco Mobley."

"Who is DeMarco, Zori?"

"Just a guy from school."

Mom stared at me so hard, my face burned. "So you went to the dance with Jay and you left with this guy. That is unacceptable. I did not teach you to be some skank."

"Jay didn't see me with nobody."

Jay turned to me. "I didn't have to see you. One of my friends saw you and DeMarco at the Waffle House."

Dang, this dude was really snitching. He was really telling everything he knew. But he was hurt and I could see it in his face. I was sorry and I couldn't justify my actions any longer.

I looked Mom in her eyes and said, "Mom, Jay is telling you the truth. What I did was wrong." I turned to Jay and said, "Jay, I'm very sorry. I hope you can one day find it in your heart to forgive me."

There was a long awkward silence. I looked at Jay and then I turned to Mom. She now had a disappointed look on her face.

"Apology accepted," Jay said.

Mom hugged Jay. "I am so sorry, Jay that this happened to you."

"Not your fault, Ms. Neal," he said, then left. I didn't want him to leave. Wished he could stay for a few more hours 'cause I knew that once he was gone, I was gonna get chewed out big time.

Mom's eyes were intense. She didn't say a word and the silence was killing me. I wished she'd just get it over with and chew me out. I could take the cursing, but not the hard stares. The disappointment. What would my punishment be? Maybe she would take the car. My phone. Whatever it was, I needed her to tell me now. I couldn't take it anymore.

I broke the ice. "Mom, I know you're mad and I'm sorry. This will not happen again."

She put her hands on my shoulders and shook me hard. She had never hit me, but the look in her eyes told me that she would backhand if she got mad enough. I took a step away from her, waiting on her to go off. I needed her to go off. I needed her to get it out of her system.

"Mom, I'm sorry."

She paced angrily. "You're right, you're sorry. One sorry little heifer. This boy got his dad to rent a stretch limo for this dance. This ain't even the prom but just a regular dance and this is what you do, behave like some chicken head."

"I'm not a chicken head."

"Yeah, chicken heads know better than you."

My mind went back to the night. I thought about the drinking in the back of the limo. Thought about the alcohol I had with Adrianna. I was not a drinker. Maybe the alcohol had impaired my judgment. I wanted to tell Mom I was under the influence and perhaps that made me behave the way I did. But that would have been worse. I could not tell this woman that I had taken a few drinks. Could not tell her I might have been drunk. This would have made it worse. God, the only thing that could be worse than her finding out that I had been drinking was if she found out what had happened to Adrianna. That could not happen. Ever.

"What is wrong with you, Zori?" she asked. I

could only see the whites of her eyes and this made me nervous.

"Nothing is wrong." I turned away from her stare. My mind raced. I needed an excuse but there was none. I had just done what I had wanted to do.

"Who is this boy you left with?"

"I didn't leave with anybody."

She gave me that look again.

My eyes met Mom's. I hesitated before speaking. "Look, Mom, DeMarco didn't go to the dance. He had gotten a room at the hotel."

"Okay, let me get this straight. You break curfew coming in the house after midnight. You go to the dance with one boy and leave with another. You go to a room with a boy. I'm assuming you had sex, too. The only thing you didn't do was get drunk."

I didn't have sex with him but in her mind she was going to believe that I did have sex. It was only logical. I mean, I did leave the dance and go to a hotel room with a boy. Who does that unless they're going to have sex? But the truth was that I didn't have sex, I only fell asleep in DeMarco's arms. Jimmy came the closest to having sex.

"DeMarco. Now why does his name sound so familiar?"

I was silent. I knew why his name sounded familiar, but I didn't want to remind her. I knew if she thought about it long enough it would come to her.

"Zori, why does DeMarco's name sound familiar? Do I know him?"

214 Might as well connect the pieces for her. I just wanted this whole scene to be over already. "Yeah, he was the boy that took me shopping."

"The boy that took you shopping." She was almost screaming now.

"Yeah."

"A boy that I have never ever met, but yet you're going to hotel rooms with him?"

"Mom, you make it sound so bad."

"There is nothing right about my sixteen-year-old daughter going to a hotel room with a boy."

I decided that I had to speak up for myself, I had to let her know the truth. Well, not the part about Adrianna and Jimmy, but I had to let her know that nothing happened, so she could calm down about this whole room thing. "Mom, nothing happened. All we did was watch tv, then go to the Waffle House."

"You expect me to believe that, Zori? I know why people get rooms, I was a girl before. A girl that dealt with boys."

"It's the truth."

"Zori, I'm not going to be a grandmother just yet. I am not ready to be a grandmother."

"Mom, you're not going to be a grandmother."

She shook her head. "I hope you know that you really messed up this time."

"Yeah."

"You know it would have been better if you

Kevin Elliott

didn't go out with Jay at all. That would have been better than to go out with him and leave. That was really poor character."

215

"Mom, I'm sorry." I looked her in her disappointed eyes. She looked like she had failed as a parent. She had taught me better and I knew better, but I had chosen not to do better.

She hugged me and said, "Go to your room and bring me that cell phone. There will be no hanging out on the weekends for a month."

"A whole month?"

"And I'm taking your car, meaning that you'll be catching the bus to school."

"The bus?"

She gave me a look that said I was pressing my luck. Mom really wanted to punish me longer than that. I could tell and actually I had expected a harsher punishment than that. My cell phone would be gone for a month. I would have to text DeMarco and Candace from Yahoo Messenger, and Jay, well he was gone for good. I reflected back on that night and it had actually started out pretty good. Jay wasn't as stuffy as I'd thought he'd be. He'd looked very handsome and he'd actually made me a tad bit jealous. Like Jamie Foxx said, blame it on the alcohol . . . that Mom would never know about. Thank God Jay didn't snitch about that. If he had snitched about that, he would have had to snitch on himself.

I went to my room and got my cell phone, deleting all my text messages before I handed it

SWAG

over. When I returned to give it to Mom, she asked, "How in the world did a teenager get a hotel room?"

"I don't know. I think his brother got it for him." Did I just say too much?

"I know what happens in rooms and I know you weren't in the room playing monopoly. I need more info on this boy. You told me his mom was dead, but where is his father?"

"I don't think his father is in his life. His older brothers are raising him."

"How did you get tied up with him?"

"I like him, he's cool, he's smart. Just because he don't live with his parents don't make him a bad person, Mom."

"I didn't say he was."

There was an awkward silence again. Then she said, "Go to your room and think about your actions. I am hurt and embarrassed by your behavior. I've taught you better and you need to act like it."

Finally dismissed, I rushed to my room to get away from my mom's disappointment. I hoped that she'd keep this whole episode to herself, 'cause I didn't want to have to deal with my dad, too.

# 8

——

Being without my cell phone was brutal. I could catch up with some of my friends on my computer on twitter, but there was nothing that could replace my cell phone. Nothing. Sometimes I would forget that I didn't have it and check my purse. It was the worst in the morning when I would roll over and look for it. I was glad I deleted all my texts and told all my friends, including DeMarco, that I didn't have my cell phone, just in case they wanted to text something weird to my phone. When I saw Jay at school, he looked in my direction but didn't acknowledge me and it was killing me inside to see somebody who'd liked me, now didn't want to have anything to do with me. I was now a bad person in his view. After the second period bell rang I walked past him again.

This time I stopped him. "Can I talk to you for a sec?"

The look on his face said: Are you serious? I dare you.

"Just one second, I promise you it will not take long."

"Okay."

"Hey, I just wanted to say that I'm sorry."

"You said that at your house and I accepted your apology."

"But I want you to believe me."

He took a deep breath and said, "Look Zori, are you really sorry or are you sorry because your mom knows what you did?"

"Jay I'm sorry, really I am, I am not that kind of person. What I did to you was wrong and nobody should have had to go through what I took you through."

"What really pissed me off about the whole situation is that I asked you were you seeing DeMarco, but you kept saying no."

"But I did say we'd gone out on dates."

"You should have told me it was kind of serious, you should have told me that you liked him."

What Jay was saying was right. I should have been respectful enough to tell Jay that I liked DeMarco. I don't know why I couldn't bring myself to just tell the truth. I guess part of me liked Jay. Part of me knew that Jay was the type of boy that I should be with.

I stared at the floor for a moment and when I

realized it I looked up into his eyes. They were sad. My apology really was heartfelt, and I wanted him to believe me. I just didn't want thcsc to be just words.

He extended his hand and when we shook hands he held my hand for a long time. Our pulses were in sync. He smiled and his eyes became a little bit happier. He finally said, "I forgive you Zori."

I smiled and said, "Thank you Jay." I walked away feeling a little bit better about the situation. Not because I had offered a sincere apology, but because Jay had really forgiven me.

After school, I ran into DeMarco walking into the student parking lot. He was just about to hop in the truck when I called his name. He turned, smiled, and leaned up against the truck.

"So, you hanging out with me today."

"You know I'm grounded."

"So how does that grounded thing work?"

I laughed because I knew he couldn't be serious. He knew what being grounded meant. Everybody did, well everybody who had been grounded. When I saw that his face was serious, I realized there was a possibility that DeMarco had never been grounded before. I mean how could he? Why would he? Who would ground him? He didn't have a mother and I knew his drug dealing brothers darn sure wouldn't ground him.

"Being grounded means I can't go anywhere after school."

"Okay, but why don't you have a phone?"

"She took that away, too. It's part of my punishment."

"Your mom is tripping. That ain't even fair."

"It ain't supposed to be fair."

He pulled me to him. I was now positioned between his legs. I looked around. I didn't want any of the faculty or staff to see me up on him like that. That would be all I needed to get caught kissing at school with DeMarco. Mom would really flip.

He put his hand around my waist and I leaned into him briefly before I pulled away.

"What's wrong, shorty?"

"Now you know we ain't supposed to be kissing here. What if we get caught?"

"Everybody kisses at school."

"Look, I ain't trying to be grounded till next Christmas."

"Your mom is hardcore, huh."

"She's being a parent."

"She's going overboard with this whole thing."

He still looked confused. DeMarco was a guy who had disrespected many people and he didn't think there was anything wrong with what I done. In his eyes, this behavior was perfectly normal.

"I wanted to hang out this Friday. My brother is going to let me hold his Benz."

"Well, I can't." I looked him in the eye. He looked sad, but his sadness didn't pull at me the way I thought it would. What had changed? "You know I want to hang out, but I can't."

He hugged me. "This month will be over before you know it."

"I hope so."


After school I was en route to the bus when I heard Candace call my name. She was behind me. I turned and faced her.

She asked, "Where are you going?"

"Home." Duh!

"The student parking lot is the other way."

"I'm catching the bus home. Mom took the car away."

"Come on, you can ride with me."

I was hesitant at first for two reasons. The first reason: me and Candace haven't been on the best of terms lately. Reason number two: I knew she was going to lecture me about what happened and try to make herself out to be holier than thou, but this is the same chick that was sexing a college dude.

"Come on. You know you don't wanna ride the bus."

She was right about that. Once you've stopped riding the bus, you don't want to go back. It was like moving from a nice neighborhood to the hood. I followed her to her car.

There was silence in the car for about three minutes. Finally, she said, "I hope you're not going to still see that thug."

"Come on, I don't need another mama. Is this why you asked me to ride with you?"

"No, of course not. I missed having my best friend in my life." She smiled, and I have to admit that I was hoping she'd meet me halfway in repairing our friendship. I never imagined that a guy would cause this much trouble between us.

I had really missed Candace, too and I was glad that we had made up, but she wasn't my mom and I really didn't like her telling me what I should and shouldn't be doing. Without her comments, it was becoming clear to me that DeMarco was not the guy that I need to be seeing. The whole thrill about seeing a bad boy was wearing off, and I knew I couldn't keep hiding it from Mom. It wasn't right and it seemed that as soon as I told one lie, I would have to cover that lie up with another one. And it had become clear to me that DeMarco was not going to stop hanging out with Lil Jimmy, the future sex offender, and that told me a lot about him. Mom always said you are the company you keep. But I swear, part of me loved that boy. I don't know why I did. I just did.

Candace glanced at me long enough for our eyes to meet, then she looked back to the road ahead. The speed limit was thirty-five near the school. We were going about twenty-five, so her mind was definitely not on the road.

"Candace, I know I messed up," I said. I had apologized to Jay and I had told Mom I was wrong. I didn't feel like going over why I was wrong with Candace. I just wanted to move past this situation.

"Zori, this is not about you messing up, this is about how you could possibly lose everything if you go to jail with this clown."

"What do you think? That I go on drug runs with DeMarco. Come on, are you serious?" She was really playing me now, like I was some naive. My mind went back to the day me and DeMarco was in the parking lot and I discovered the bags of weed in his book bag. But there was no way I would ever be that stupid, to be with DeMarco when he was making his drug deals. He never even talked about drugs to me and that may have been one of the reasons I liked him.

Candace pulled over by the side of the road and turned to me. "I care about you, that's all."

"And I care about me."

"What is that supposed to mean?"

"Don't judge me, that's what that's supposed to mean. You're no better than I am."

"I didn't say I was."

"Good, because at least I was never with a guy in his twenties."

"He's a good guy though."

"He's an old guy, too old for you."

Candace sighed. I could see she was angry. I knew Candace loved me and she had made some good points, but I really didn't want to hear her good points.

"Look, Candace, I'm sorry for bringing Barry up, but I swear to you everything is good with me. Nothing is going to happen to me."

A few minutes went by with neither of us saying anything. I decided to make the first move and pulled Candace to me for a hug.

I texted DeMarco from yahoo messenger. He didn't respond, maybe it was because it was from yahoo messenger and not a phone number. About an hour later, he texted back: Who this?

Zori

DeMarco: Oh, my bad

Me: You know I don't have a phone man, come on, who else is gonna be texting you from Yahoo Messenger?

DeMarco: True dat, so what's up, shorty?

Me: Nothing much stuck in this house and Mom is getting on my last nerve, waiting on her to leave so I can at least get on the home phone.

DeMarco: Where is she going?

Me: Some dinner banquet from her job

DeMarco: You should hang out with me

Me: No. I can't hang with you, you know I can't leave the house.

DeMarco: Your mom is gonna be gone. I will have you back before she comes back

Me: You don't know when she's coming back, now how you know you're gonna have me back

DeMarco: 'Cause I know

Me: Not a good answer

DeMarco: Come on man, live life a little

Me: I'm not a man and I ain't about to get in any more trouble

DeMarco: I feel ya

The longer I sat there looking at the screen, the more I began to see it DeMarco's way. With my mom gone to the dinner for at least three hours, she'd never know I'd left the house. It wasn't like she'd stop talking to folks and get up from the table to call me. And I did want to see DeMarco, just one more time before I dropped him. Of course, I couldn't have him come pick me up—the neighbors would definitely notice him—but maybe Candace could come get me . . . scratch that. Candace would have a fit if I mentioned DeMarco to her, and I didn't want to mess up our friendship again. I'll get Malaka to take me over to DeMarco's brother's spot for a few minutes. I still remembered where his brother lived. Yeah, I would go over there and surprise him. I'd get me a good-bye kiss and get back to the house.

Mom left at 7:30, and Malaka's green Honda Accord pulled up at 8. I was dressed and I looked good, if I do say so myself. I wore some extra tight skinny jeans and heels, and make up was done to perfection.

I stepped out the front door and looked around. Even though I was heading out with Malaka, I didn't want to boldly stroll outside if the neighbors were in their yards. When I saw Mr. Harry across the street peeping Malaka's car, I knew I'd made a good decision by not having DeMarco come over. Mr. Harry seeing me with one of my girls shouldn't be worth sharing. And if he did tell mom that Malaka came over, I'd just tell her that I borrowed Malaka's textbook. I signaled for Malaka to back the car a little farther up the driveway so I could hop in unnoticed.

"You look amazing."

"Thank you, chica."

I told her where DeMarco's brother lived and we were there five minutes later. I didn't see the Escalade, but DeMarco said he would be there today, so I hopped out of the car and knocked on the door. Nobody answered. Was I wrong? Suddenly, I felt like a fool for just popping up. I went back to the car and asked Malaka for her cell phone so I could call DeMarco. She was about to pass it to me when the Escalade rolled up. The first thing I noticed was the chick on the passenger side. I didn't freak out, there had to be a reasonable explanation for this. This had to be a sister or a cousin. This couldn't be his girl. He was dating me; I hadn't dumped him yet.

DeMarco looked like he was trying to figure out what was going on. I guess he didn't recognize Malaka's car and he hadn't seen me yet. He jumped out of the Escalade, and so did the girl.

Kevin Elliott

I got out of Malaka's car smiling, still thinking that the girl couldn't be anything but a friend.

DeMarco frowned. "What are you doing here?"

I didn't like his tone, but I was gonna let it slide for now. "I wanted to surprise you, baby."

The girl said, "Baby?" Then looked at me and said, "Who are you?"

With that, I knew she wasn't a friend or cousin. Looking at her busted shoes and last season's bebe dress, I also knew she had no class. She was cute, but her weave definitely needed to be upgraded. She had nothing on me, but if this is what he wanted, fine.

"DeMarco, what is going on?" the girl said.

He didn't answer, he didn't even look her way. Instead, he made direct eye contact with me and said, "What are you doing here?"

My heart raced a little. This is not how I wanted this scene to go down.

"Who is this girl?" the girl asked again.

DeMarco turned to the girl and said, "Hey, I don't owe anybody no kind of explanation." Turning to me, he said, "Nobody is my girlfriend."

I said, "Good-bye, DeMarco."

"Go," he said, as if he were dismissing me. "I don't give a care if you leave. This is what you get when you pop up at people's house unannounced."

This was the same nonchalant attitude he'd had the day I confronted him when he was with

Christian. That should have been the last day I saw him, but instead I gave him another chance. I walked into that hotel room, even though I saw he was with Lil Jimmy, his sex offender friend. I thought about how I had sacrificed being with Jay to be with him. Jay was a good person. He would never do anything trifling like this. I was here to dismiss DeMarco, not the other way around. I should have seen this coming.

I walked away slowly. Before I got back in the car, I turned and said, "No, this is what you get when you believe that a fool is gonna change." My eyes had teared up. Malaka gave me a hug before we drove away.

I exploded midway through the ride. I felt myself fall completely apart. I had never allowed anybody to get to me like that. Reality set in: the relationship was never really real. While I was dating DeMarco, he was keeping his options open. He didn't say I was his girl, but I wanted to believe I was his girl. But I wasn't. Neither was the other girl. DeMarco was a player and I had been played, the same way I'd played Jay.

The next morning, Candace drove me to school. We rode in silence for most of the way. I was lost in thought about DeMarco, and hoped that Candace didn't bring up his name.

After a while Candace asked, "Is something wrong?"

"Nothing is wrong," I lied. I really didn't want

to get into a discussion about DeMarco. Didn't want to sound stupid.

"Come on, you know I know you." Candace said.

More silence. I knew Malaka was going to tell her eventually.

We drove five more minutes, then she said, "Okay, you don't want to talk about it, I totally understand."

"There is nothing to talk about."

"Really?"

Her voice was very condescending.

I turned to her and said, "Candace, I don't want to hear a bunch of I told you so's."

"This has something to do with DeMarco?"

"It has everything to do with DeMarco." I dropped my head.

She pulled the car over and turned to me. "It's gonna be okay."

I burst into tears again. I couldn't control myself.

Candace squeaked, "What did he do? Did he get you pregnant?"

I composed myself. I got a Kleenex from my purse. "No, thank God."

"What happened?"

"Me and Malaka went to his house on Friday . . . and DeMarco drove up with another girl in the car."

"No, he didn't!" she exclaimed. "You must've been devastated."

"The girl must have been somebody to him because she kept asking who I was."

"Guys like that are not the marrying type. They are the player type. My momma says guys like that will break your heart."

"Don't I know that. I learned a tough lesson. I just wish I would have given Jay a fair chance. Wish I didn't like DeMarco so much."

Candace said. "And trust me, he now wishes he didn't like you so much. There will be other guys, others that will treat you with respect."

I smiled. I loved my best friend. Loved that she knew exactly what to say and what time to say it.

In the student parking lot, I heard somebody call out my name. I turned and looked: it was DeMarco.

I kept walking like I didn't hear him. He got out of his truck and ran and caught up with me and Candace. I continued to ignore him, until he got in front of me so I would have to stop.

Candace stopped and said, "Leave her alone." She got between us and grabbed my hand. Together we walked past DeMarco.

"I need to talk to you for a moment, shorty."

"She don't want to talk to you," Candace said.

"Candace you stay out of this," he said walking behind us.

"You heard my friend. I don't want to talk to you."

"I just want to apologize."

"Apology accepted." We kept it moving.

"Give me two minutes."

In my heart and my head, I knew I was over him, but there was something deep inside that wanted to hear what he had to say. Hearing him admit his mistake would be gratifying. I whispered to Candace, "I want to hear what he has to say." I could tell she wanted to say no, but she nodded and agreed to wait for me. She stepped a few feet away.

All of a sudden, DeMarco looked a little nervous, as if he was trying to figure out what he wanted to say. I wasn't trying to draw this out, so I snapped, "I have to go to class, so hurry."

"Listen, I just wanted to say that girl was nobody to me."

"Come on don't give me that B.S. You didn't say that in front of her."

He avoided looking at my eyes—the sign of a liar. "I didn't know what to say." He paused, then continued, "Listen, shorty, we never said we were a couple."

"We sure didn't, so really there is no need to apologize."

"I feel guilty."

"For what?"

"'Cause you're a good person."

"Thank you," I said. I knew I was a good person, but I knew I hadn't been doing good things lately. And it all started when I started talking to DeMarco. I know I couldn't place all the blame on him, but before DeMarco, I'd never associated with a guy who attacked women, I never drank, I didn't tell my mom crazy lies, stood up a nice guy at a dance, or had a guy I like play me for a fool. But I guess compared to this liar, I was a good person, and compared to Osama bin Laden, he was a good person.

"I'm really sorry. I shouldn't have played with you. You deserve better. Actually you're too good for me."

"Again your apology is accepted. No hard feelings, just a lesson learned, my friend."

He offered his hand. I shook it.

Me and Candace walked away. He walked back in the direction of the student parking lot. He was probably ditching today.

The next day, when Candace and I pulled up to school the police had the parking lot blocked off. And there were at least six police cars there, including a K-9 unit and police van. Not good.

A tall officer with red hair and freckled face barked orders. "Park across the street."

We both wondered what had happened. "I hope nobody got hurt."

"Me too," I said. You never could tell. Killings on school campuses were almost common occurrences. I just hoped nothing like that was happening at my school.

After parking the car across the street, we walked back toward campus with a guy named

Derrick Jones. Candace asked him what was going on.

"They busted this dude with weed, man. And a gun."

Candace and I looked at each other. Neither of us said a word, but I know we were thinking about the same person.

"What did he look like?"

"Tall dude, used to play on the basketball team and drives an Escalade."

I shook my head. "DeMarco?"

"Yeah, that's him," Derrick said. "They got the dude in cuffs and everything. Somebody must have snitched on him."

"Wow," was all I could say.

"I feel bad for the dude. He looked like he wanted to cry, but that's what happens when you do stuff like that. You gotta be prepared for the worst."

Candace said, "I don't feel bad for him. Do the crime, pay the time."

But I felt bad for him. I knew DeMarco. He wasn't a bad person, he just made bad decisions. At that moment, I was so glad that we'd called it quits and that I'd made peace with him. I couldn't imagine getting caught up with him and getting arrested. My dreams of going to college would have dissipated. I said a prayer for him, and thanked God for sparing me this embarrassment.

# 9

————

Two months had passed since DeMarco's arrest.
I hadn't seen or heard anything from him. It's
almost like he didn't exist.

Then I got a letter from him.

*Shorty, I hope all is well with you.*

*I'm sure you heard about what hap-
pened to me. Well, after they arrested me,
they never let me out because I was already
on probation. The judge sentenced me to six
months juvenile detention. Probably the
best thing that could have happened to me,
because after being around dudes with
nothing on their mind, I now realize my potential. Most of the guys in here can't even
read on an eighth grade level, and I'm like,
man I don't belong here. But I do belong*

*here, if that makes any sense. I belong here because I did something wrong. I get to reflect and get my priorities in order. The coach came to visit me. He says he can get me back in school, and he wants me to live with him and his wife. I may take him up on his offer. I love my brothers, but they are bad news, a bad influence on me. I am just so happy somebody is going to give me a second chance. I'm so happy people still believe in me. I hope everything is going well with you. Just wanted to say I always considered you a very good person and friend and I hope we can resume our friendship when I'm released. We'll be just friends, 'cause I know you've probably moved on and I respect that. Also, just wanted to say Jay is a good guy and you should try to make it work with him. I like him, and I think he would be good for you. Guys like me don't make good boyfriends until we grow up and sometimes it takes something like this to make us grow up. See you in four months.*

*DeMarco*

I read the letter again. Not because I was glad to hear from him, but because it seemed like he had matured a lot. It seemed as though he had learned his lesson. And I think DeMarco was sent to me for me to learn a lesson. And as far as me being with Jay, that will never happen. I'm not thinking about boyfriends. I'm focusing on me and being the best me I can be. No boyfriend for me, no sex for me, and no liquor for me.

Don't miss Nikki Carter's

*Doing My Own Thing.*

Available now wherever books are sold!

Have you ever been super nervous about something for absolutely no reason at all?

Today is the day we get to see the episodes of our BET reality show, *Backstage: The Epsilon Records Summer Tour.* I shouldn't be nervous, because I went out of my way to make sure I didn't do anything that could be misconstrued as ghetto or lame. I didn't talk bad about anybody in my confessionals, I never once used profanity, and I was only digging one boy the whole time (Sam).

So, I shouldn't be nervous.

But for some crazy reason I am. I have the butterflies-flitting-in-the-pit-of-my-stomach feeling that something ridiculous is about to pop off.

Maybe it's because I haven't really talked to anyone except Sam since the taping completed. We ended on a bad note. The final show in New

York City got cancelled because of a botched kidnapping attempt that ended up in a nightclub brawl. It was all bad.

I keep playing the whole thing over and over again in my head, because I knew about the kidnapping ahead of time, but didn't tell anyone. In hindsight, I should've tried to do something, but I was afraid that something bad might happen to my mom and little cousin. That's all I was thinking about. It didn't even occur to me that telling Big D, Mystique, or Dilly about what was going down could've given a different result.

And now, I'm paying the price for that. Dilly's still not speaking to me, and the tour has been over for three weeks. Big D is a little salty with me too, and that really hurts, because he's always in my corner. Mystique is a little disappointed, but she told me that she would've done what I did, so that made me feel better.

My phone buzzes on my hip. "Hey, Sam."

"You want me to pick you up to go to the studio? Or are you driving, since you finally decided to stop being a tightwad and got yourself a car?"

I laugh out loud. Yes, I am a tightwad with the money I've earned so far on the songwriting end of things. But when I got my six-thousand-dollar check at the end of the tour, I went to a used-car lot and got a car. It's a tricked-out gold Toyota Camry that was probably seized from a drug dealer or something. Anyhoo, I'm on wheels.

"Why don't I pick you up for a change?" I ask. "I

do want to drive, but I don't want to show up alone. I'm afraid I might get jumped."

"Dilly still isn't talking, huh?"

"No, and neither are Dreya and Truth, although I don't know why they're mad."

"Does Drama *need* a reason?"

I chuckle. "No, not really, but I think if someone would call her by her real name every now and then she might remember that Drama is a stage name, and that she doesn't have to live up to it."

"She will forever be Ms. Drama to me," Sam states.

"Well, whatever. She's Dreya to me. I'll pick you up in an hour. Cool?"

"Yep."

My mother calls me from the living room. "Sunday! Come here, now!"

"Sam, let me call you back. My mom is tripping on something."

Her voice sounds crazy, like she's about to try to ground me for something. But we've officially halted all punishment activities since I turned eighteen, and graduated from high school. Like how's she gonna ground me when I'm helping pay bills up in here? Real talk.

But still she sounds like she's in trip-out mode. I am sooo not in the mood.

"Sunday, sit down," my mom says when I come into the living room.

"What's up?"

"Look at what just came in the mail."

She hands me an envelope that's addressed to me and my mom, but doesn't have a return address. I open up the envelope and inside is a cashier's check.

For twenty-five thousand dollars.

It's the exact amount of money that my mother's boyfriend Carlos borrowed from my college fund to buy into Club Pyramids. It's the exact amount that was stolen from him when the deal went sour and he ended up getting shot.

"Do you think this has anything to do with Carlos's cousins trying to kidnap Dilly?" she asks.

"How can we say for sure? We don't even know who sent it."

My mother replies, "It had to be Carlos. Somehow he got his hands on the money and he's trying to make it up to you."

"But why wouldn't he let you know it was coming? I mean, he knows how to get in contact with us."

My mother sits down next to me and takes the check back. She flips it over a few times as if she's looking for clues to its origin. She sighs and shakes her head.

"Maybe it was the record company. Maybe they want all of the ghettoness surrounding you to stop, especially since they want to do a reality show with just you."

Apparently, BET liked what they saw of me from

the reality-show footage, and they want to give me my own show. That's all good, and I know they don't want any more brawls taking place during my new gig. But how would the head honchos at BET know about the twenty-five thousand dollars? There is no way Mystique or Big D would tell them what *really* went down at the club in New York.

"I don't think it was Epsilon Records, Mommy. They aren't really in the loop with all the drama."

"Maybe it was Big D or Mystique?"

I bite my lip and think about this for a moment. Big D is out. He's known all along about the money, and if he wanted to give it to me, he could've done it at any time. Mystique is a possibility. She's the type who would do something under the radar and not sign her name to it.

"I don't know," I finally reply. "Maybe. I'll ask them both."

My mother shakes her head. "No. Don't ask. Whoever sent this doesn't want it to be known, or else they would've signed their name. We just have to look at it for exactly what it is."

"And what's that?" I ask, completely confused at her reasoning.

"That's simple. It's a gift from God."

Hmmm . . . a gift from God? While I'm as Christian as the next person, I doubt that He's just sending random checks in the mail. If He was doing that, why doesn't He send them to people who really need it? I mean, for real, I've got hundreds of thousands of dollars on the way. Isn't there some poor single mom out there who could use the check more? I'm just saying.

But there's no way I'm gonna argue with my mother when it has to do with a blessing. She'll make me attend daily revivals, Bible study, vacation Bible school and everything else if I even think I sound like I don't have faith.

So, it's up to me to figure out the identity of the mystery check writer. Something new to put on my already overflowing plate!

"Well, I guess we just need to thank the Lord," I reply.

"You sound like you're being sarcastic, Sunday."

"I'm not! If it's from God, then I think I should thank Him."

"All right. Keep it up and your new reality show will follow you around at vacation Bible school."

This would be funny only if she didn't really mean it. Even though I'm eighteen, I'm still afraid of her. I have to hurry up and figure out who the mystery check donor is, before my mom makes her move.

Can somebody say a prayer for me?